ADVANCE PRAISE FOR *PRIMROSE STREET*

"Reed wove together joys, sorrows, relationships, and struggles in a way that was both informative and profound. The effect has lingered in ways that continue to draw me to find parallels all around me. I did not want to put the book down; this will be a book I will return to many times over."

—Marion Boyd, psychotherapist, grief counsellor

"A colourful group of characters drew me into this thoughtful story of a group of neighbours and kept me reading right until the end! Twisted together and pulled apart, new connections being made; it was a well woven tale yet seemingly believable. It was so real in parts that I cried, the human experience was well documented. Reading *Primrose Street* had me thinking about my kids, my parents, and my own relationships. The subject matter is provocative, and makes *Primrose Street* a very interesting glimpse into the minds of people with different lifestyle choices and experiences. I will be recommending this book to my book club, and I'm sure it will spark a lot of lively discussion!"

—Jen Hawkins, photographer, nurse

To Jill,

To thine own self be true. Enjoy, Marina Reed

marinalreed.com

Primrose Street

Copyright 2018 by Marina L. Reed

ISBN: 978-1-988279-69-5

All rights reserved

Editor: Allister Thompson

Published in Stratford, Canada, by Blue Moon Publishers.

The author greatly appreciates you taking the time to read this work. Please consider leaving a review wherever you bought the book, or telling your friends or blog readers about *Primrose Street* to help spread the word. Thank you for your support.

PRIMROSE STREET

MARINA L. REED

BlueMoon
PUBLISHERS

To Mitchel Reed. You are a blessing.

CONTENTS

ACKNOWLEDGEMENTS

I'd like to thank my son, Mitchel. His inspiration, artistic vision, encouragement, critiques, and support have been unwavering. He would not let me give up! He brainstormed with me, listened, and hugged me when I was overwhelmed — hugs and kisses. To all my friends who support and encourage me each day, you are my sunshine. Thank you all. To Allister, who tells me hard truths with a soft edge and makes me think and think again, I am grateful. Rachel Sentes, thank you for picking up the oar and jumping in the boat with me. And to Blue Moon, for the chance to realize my dream. There are no words!! For all who walk down Primrose Street, thank you for joining me on this journey. I hope it will be the beginning of many as we enrich each other's lives. xo

PRIMROSE STREET – FAMILY "TREE"

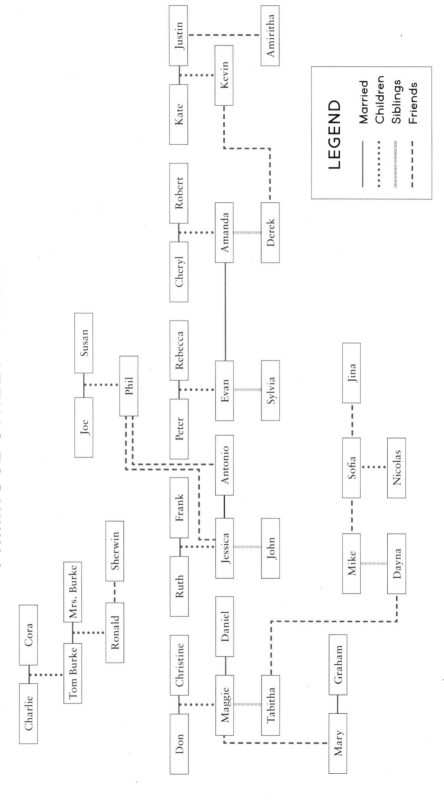

The maple trees have watched over the residents of Primrose Street for almost a hundred years. They stand steadfastly along the street, in front of homes, in backyards, some more gnarled than others. Their branches hang over lawns and shade the driveways. They are climbing projects for children, homes for birds and squirrels. Some of their long limbs have been shamelessly amputated by hydro workers for electrical lines to run unimpeded along the street. A few of them have become hollowed by sadness and were taken down completely, unable to recover, their stumps now used for planters or decorative art. The trees protect in their quiet way, taking deep breaths as residents move through generations.

A new family recently moved into Eleven Primrose Street. It is an older home with a big, fenced backyard that supports a treehouse, a small shed for tools and lawn cutting gear, and a small fountain centred around a flower garden. There is a rounded, glassed-in front porch with a few garden chairs and a table. It is an elegant entrance to the older home. It is there that Sofia, a young mother, keeps watch over her young son, Nicolas. He has firmly planted himself beside the trunk of the maple outside Twelve Primrose Street, refusing to go home. She carefully peeks through the glass, watching his tantrum. The boy presses his head against the bark of the maple while his big German Shepherd sits protectively beside him, waiting for the wailing to stop. Nicolas eventually pulls himself up, using the tree for support, and the dog regally rises and waits. The boy wraps his chubby fingers around the dog's collar, and Merlin leads the way safely across the road and home. Sofia stays behind the glass until the two boys are safely in the house through the back door. She never lets him know she is watching. She knows Merlin would never leave Nicolas's side.

Mrs. Burke, who lives at Twelve Primrose, pulls her cream-coloured sheers to one side when she hears the wailing. She is always a bit aghast that Nicolas's mother would just let him sit by the tree alone, so she watches to make sure he gets home safely. The tantrums seem to happen regularly as the three are coming back from town, bags in hand. Nicolas just doesn't want to go home. Curiosity as to why eats away at Mrs. Burke. But it is the dog she loves. Merlin is the real star. Mrs. Burke would love a dog like that to help her. It is getting a bit difficult to navigate her porch steps, and she doesn't like having to use her cane. Ronald, her grandson who will be nine years old this year, has a black-and-white Border Collie, but he is very excitable and exhausts Mrs. Burke every time they visit. Kevin, who lives next door to her, has a lovely St. Bernard named Paddy. Even with all the drooling, the dog is so peaceful. Kevin is a very sulky, lazy teenager. He is tall, on the heavy side, with a mop of curly brown hair. He often just sits on his front porch smoking something illegal, and Paddy patiently lies at his feet. It had been a scandal when Kevin's mother walked out. Everyone thought they were such a lovely couple, such a lovely family. Justin had married young when Kate said she was pregnant; he is just that kind of man. Mrs. Burke pulled a lot of sheer curtains back that spring and made a lot of casseroles for Justin. It has been a few years now, but Kevin still seems to be in a state of shock.

And then there is Graham, whose wife died very suddenly of cancer the same year Kate walked out on her family. He lives down at Twenty-Five Primrose and owns the bakery and cheese shop in town. Twenty-Five Primrose is a small house, board and batten, that Graham renovated into a charming kind of cottage. He treated the outside wood with a rustic blue paint and trimmed all the windows with white shutters. His wife had created a beautiful flower garden in the front that bloomed from April to October. There were often garden competitions between her and Rebecca, who lives across the road. Graham faithfully keeps her garden weed-free since her death and tends to the house, but it was easy to tell that his heart was shredded by her death. Even with all that, he is still the go-to guy.

Everyone on the street goes to Graham if they have a house issue; he just seems to be able to fix anything. And he is nice enough always to try.

His shop is on the main street in Martineville. The street has a small but eclectic collection of food shops and clothing selections. People can still go to a local butcher for their meat, the shoemaker to fix all footwear, fresh bread and imported cheeses at Graham's, a flower shop, a wine store, fruit and vegetable fair, a dry cleaner, a dollar store, and one cinema. It has everything anyone could need. At the end of town are some box stores, a larger grocery store, and a small satellite university campus from the larger university in the city an hour away. The enrolment at the university in the big city was growing so fast, and there was no space to expand, so a new campus was created in Martineville. That was good news for Martineville and for foreign students. Amiritha Desai is one such student. She came from Pakistan to continue with her engineering degree. When the university told her it was moving her classes to the campus in Martineville, she was less than impressed. She liked the big city and had a nice place there. But to her most pleasant surprise, she found a much nicer apartment in Martineville for half the price she was paying before, and she is beginning to enjoy the luxury of a small town. She is even finding hints of love here.

It isn't just the campus that educates. The local library offers classes for everyone, of every age. Rebecca often gives courses on flower care and gardening. She created such a beautiful garden of her own and read many books to get it that way. Now she likes to help others with bloom-a-mania. And then on Wednesday morning, the local quilting bee meets. That's where Mrs. Burke heard that maybe love has come back into Graham's life.

MAIN STREET

The Gouda cheese was too bland. She tried it last week. Mary was looking for something with more of a smoky, nutty flavour — a cheese that could stand alone with a glass of red wine.

She peered through the oval glass covering the cheese display, holding the small paper with the customer number she had been given when entering the store. Other shoppers were impatiently waiting, looking at watches, eyeing each other. A number was randomly bellowed over the din of voices and shoes and doors and servers. Someone would raise their number high, sweaty and crumpled, like they had just won a lottery, and move forward to select their meat for the week or cheeses. She was jostled into the man beside her and gathered her bag a little closer to her chest. She heard her number and pushed toward the front. It was like being part of a herd where the strongest survived. She explained what she wanted in a cheese, to moans and groans from customers behind.

"So choose already," someone yelled.

The server was oblivious to the herd and presented her with a slice of cheese to taste on a piece of wax paper. Spanish cheese. It rolled over and around her tongue, but no, it wasn't what she was looking for.

"Maybe a Tilsit," he offered. More groans from the herd as he prepared another piece of wax paper. Disgruntled voices arose from the restless crowd. She was rattled, getting warm in her wool coat and hat. She accepted the cheese slice, beads of nervous perspiration beginning on her temples and between her breasts. But cheese was sacred and not to be rushed. Didn't this angry mob know that? She folded the Tilsit into her mouth and felt the saliva collecting around its flavour.

"It is quite unique, but it doesn't have the nutty quality I was hoping for. I'm so sorry I can't remember its name. Maybe a Gruyère?" Someone pushed into her, jamming her up against the glass.

"Oh my God, it's only cheese. We don't have all day," someone in the mob yelled. Mary just couldn't buy cheese like this. It was like having a claw-foot bathtub filled with fragrant bubbles and only being able to dip in your toe. Her anxiousness forced the perspiration to fall around the curve of her breasts, settling in the elastic of her bra. She just took a larger slice of the Tilsit and moved through glares and jibes to the cash, wanting to leave more than she wanted the perfect cheese. Maggie would probably be back in a moment anyway. She was picking up some veggies at the shop down the street. They liked to shop on Saturday; it was their outing. Afterward, they'd get a coffee and a pastry at the local café and discuss the week. It was what friends did. She would drive in from out of town each Saturday just for shopping day. The main street in Martineville was so unique, and so was Maggie; it was worth the drive.

The herd was now pushing her toward the cash. It was not a relaxing shopping day. She frantically dug for her wallet, close to tears.

A tap on her shoulder made her jump. She cautiously turned, waiting to see another angry, impatient customer ready to hurl an insult. A first she only saw the thin slice of pale cheese on the piece of wax paper and the apron double tied in the front. She politely took the slice and looked up and up into the kindest, softest, bluest eyes she had ever seen, with a decided sparkle around the edges. She stopped breathing for a whole minute at least, the cheese hovering in midair. She didn't want the moment to end or his eyes to turn away.

"I'm sorry this has been so difficult for you. People are in quite a hurry today," he said. "I thought this might be what you were searching for," and he gestured to the piece of cheese clinging to her fingers. Mary mechanically brought the food to her mouth, not taking her eyes from his. The cheese found her tongue and burst into song.

"Perfect," was all she could manage. She tried to smile.

"Thought so." He tucked a brown-wrapped package into her bag. "It's on me. Sorry for the trouble today." She swallowed down a gulp into her suddenly dry throat and made her way out of the busy store, as if moving in the silence of a cedar bush rather than through a disgruntled herd.

She took out the package, pretending she was holding his hand, and saw his name, Graham, and his phone number written on the outside of the butcher's paper. She felt an unfamiliar energy course through her body, more than an adrenaline rush, closer to the thrill of a lightning bolt dazzling the sky out of nowhere, maybe like walking into a dark room that springs into a surprise party. She turned, and there he was at the window, arranging a display. He smiled and nodded slowly, almost in a ceremonial bow.

The maples outside Twenty-Five Primrose Street bow gently in the afternoon breezes as residents walk under their inviting arches. They feel humbled in the presence of such love and allow their leaves and branches to be soft and welcoming. A lone leaf breaks free from a thin branch, fluttering gently into Maggie's lap as she sits and observes. She picks it up and holds it between her fingers, feeling its strong suppleness. She remembers six months ago, when she and her friend Mary had met for one of their Saturday outings, and Mary bought cheese. Turns out buying cheese gets you more than just a dairy product. Maggie smiles as she watches people milling about the garden.

Graham and Mary wanted a simple, elegant wedding. And that's what they created. Everyone from Primrose Street is here. There are tables on the front lawn draped with lilac-coloured silk cloths, small bouquets of daisies smiling in each vase centred on the tables. Bottles of red and white wine wait to be enjoyed, accompanied by petite plates of different cheeses, bread chunks, and dishes of balsamic vinegar for dipping. At the request of his bride, Graham created a fountain in the front garden, which creates a peaceful ambiance for the afternoon. The back garden has similar tables, another fountain, weeping cedar trees, hollyhocks, and white wisteria climbing the fences. A modest white arch stands in the centre of the yard, adorned with thin lilac ribbon and garlands of daisies.

The bride is wearing a sleeveless, pale rose-coloured satin summer dress, her hair in ringlets down her back, and Graham looks very handsome in a black shirt with thin blue stripes, grey pleated slacks and a sapphire-blue tie. It reflects his sparkling blue eyes, especially sparkly when he looks at Mary. It is hard for him to take his eyes off her, and she is the same. It is a special thing to stand so close to two people who clearly adore each other. It is infectious. Guests move closer to their spouses or partners, wanting a slice of that feeling of connection and belonging. It is truly an occasion for love. Graham and Mary move to stand under the arch, water tripping over itself in the fountain, scents of Madonna lilies wafting across the garden. The crowd moves graciously behind them, folding themselves around the periphery of the arches, craning to see. Children are held between legs or hoisted onto shoulders. The deep voice of the minister circles over the spectators, and Graham and Mary are lost in the words they speak to each other. He reaches over and strokes her face before slipping the ring onto her finger. Afterward, he leans over and kisses her cheek.

"Hey," someone brightly calls from the crowd, "you have to wait until after for that."

The crowd titters, and Graham grins but never takes his eyes from Mary's. She smiles, the edges of her lips quivering with joy, and a tear escapes from the corner of her eye as she slides the ring onto his finger. Their hands pause, her hand over his, and oh so tenderly he places his hands on either side of her face and reaches over to kiss her lips. They linger on each other's lips until there is a collective sigh from the crowd. And then they turn, lift their clasped hands into the air, and there is a cheer. Graham pulls her close to him, his arm wrapped around her waist, and she leans her head against his chest. He kisses the top of her head, and she nestles closer. Gentle jazz plays from the speakers set up on the back porch, and people stand back, waiting for the first dance. Graham and Mary oblige, and soon everyone joins in. It is everything a wedding is dreamed to be. People dance and kiss and eat and drink and laugh and fold into chairs around tables. There are no speeches, just quiet moments between friends. The new couple circulates together, never leaving one another's side.

Kevin is secretly smoking some weed at the back fence, and his dad, Justin, is talking sweetly with a foreign woman new in town, Amiritha.

His body language suggests he has no intention of leaving her side too quickly, and as she tosses her head back, enjoying his words, she is happy to be engaged as well. Charlie and Cora hold hands, remembering how they took their vows almost sixty years ago. Charlie leans over and kisses his bride on the cheek, and Cora brings her hand there and lovingly smiles at her husband. She tells Charlie how beautifully the garden has been decorated. He nods in agreement, appreciating the transformation as well, even though he'd much prefer to be working in his shop.

Maggie thinks back to some weekend parties during her high school days, when backyards would come to life with lights and punch bowls and loud music. She had never attended a lot of parties. High school for her had been about work and opportunities. It called up a mixed bag of emotions. But when she looks up and sees Mary and Graham kissing at the request of wine glasses being clinked by cutlery, she realizes that the mixed bag didn't really matter. It was all worth it. That last night of high school, Maggie fell in love, sitting in a car on Primrose Street. The boy she had coveted for five years finally kissed her. It was after the last prom, more than ten years ago.

FIFTEEN PRIMROSE STREET: MAGGIE

Maggie always felt inside out. She stood at her locker, hanging up her light blue rain jacket that had a dusting of water droplets. Her clarinet case stood on the floor beside her while she brushed her shoulder-length hair, cut in the shag style, using the small oval mirror she had taped to the inside of her locker door, and adjusted her pleated skirt. She had a slim build but always wore slightly oversized clothes. From a young age, meal times had been stressful at home for Maggie. Her father would watch how she held her fork and comment on how many times it came to her mouth. He'd pat her stomach and say, with a smile that stretched too wide, that she should be careful of forkfuls. He called her the "blender" for the way she liked to mix her food together. And soon Maggie hated meal times, hated eating, and even though she was very thin, she felt much bigger. She felt like piles of food were placed on her fork and that she looked like pudding after eating them. She was unaware of the fact that she ate and looked more like a little bird.

Rita came up behind. Her band uniform was neat and pressed, like her hair, as usual. She wore a very pink lipstick that matched her nails. "Anyone going with you to the prom this year, Maggie?"

"I'm just trying to get through this last concert, Rita," she commented without looking up from her locker. Rita played third clarinet. She had beautiful clothes, multiple boyfriends, and perfectly styled hair.

"So, no one."

"Nope." Maggie turned and looked at her. "Still having trouble with the middle section of that Joplin piece? We need to keep that really smooth."

"I'll be okay." She gave Maggie her pressed smile and walked away, her hips bouncing the conservative skirt pleats into a sexy swing. Maggie took a deep breath. She would have liked to have been a Rita just once in her high school days. Feel a hand sliding up her skirt at prom, a tongue sliding over her teeth before class. But Maggie didn't allow her skirt to bounce in a sexy way. All those forkfuls of food made her feel like she couldn't make it bounce like that, even if she wanted to.

Maggie closed her locker, picked up her clarinet, and made her way to the band room. She loved the concert evenings and was sad this would be the last one. Where else would she ever play with a band like this one, almost a full orchestra? There were thirty students in the band with a variety of woodwinds, brass, and percussion, but no strings. That put far more pressure on the woodwinds to play those parts, especially the clarinets. A violin could bow a fast piece of music effortlessly; a clarinet player did not have the same fluidity. It was a challenge. But the band was a highlight of the school. Grade nine students hovered in the wings, waiting for graduating students to leave so they could fill their places. The band held coveted, auditioned seats.

Maggie loved the deep, full sound when all instruments were engaged and the conductor was bouncing up on his toes, his baton flicking and swishing with energy. She could get lost in the intricate sounds, swept away by the grandeur. They were the only team in the school with such elaborate uniforms: pleated grey skirts or slacks for the boys, red blazers with the school crest, white shirts, red ties, or scarves. Often the wool jackets were warm, really warm, during a concert under the intense lights, but they made them stand out. When performing at another high school that year, many people commented on the sharpness of the band's appearance and the expertise of their playing. The anxious knot in her stomach was a small price to pay for being lead clarinet with the band.

As she walked down the hall, Phil fell in step with her, rolling his large tuba case behind him. Phil was about the same height as Maggie, slender, with a mop of always unbrushed, very, very brown hair. Phil was a sweet guy. You could always count on him to give you study notes or cover you if you were late for class. And he loved the band. He played tuba, percussion, saxophone. He played in a jazz band after school. He lived for his music. But when he didn't have an instrument in his hand, Maggie always thought he looked sad, sort of lost. She would recognize that, feeling much the same herself. Phil reached into his pocket and pulled out a small joint. He always had something to take the edge off, as he'd tell you.

"Care to join me? Makes those ragtime runs a lot smoother."

"No, thanks."

"Come on, when Yvonne was lead clarinet she always took a puff, said it made things easier."

"Right, which is why I'm lead clarinet now and she was sent to Havergale boarding school. Thanks, though."

"Can you drag this to the band room for me then? I'll be there in a jif."

Maggie took the handle of the tuba and carted it off. She put Phil's tuba in the corner and heard Justin call out, "Where did he go, Maggie? I want to join him."

Maggie put her hands up, open and empty, and lifted her shoulders. "Great. Thanks. I think I know where he is, I'll be right back."

Justin. Tall, dark, handsome, smart. Maggie always hoped that he might ask her out, but he had his eye on Kate right from grade nine. Justin would succeed at whatever he chose, and Kate would go along for the ride. She looked good on his arm, but that was about it. Kate, with her blond hair, big smile, large breasts, and round eyes, could reel any guy in. Justin was such a good guy that no one had the heart to tell him. Besides, it might just work out fine.

Maggie sat down and put her clarinet together, holding the reed in her mouth to moisten it before fixing it onto the mouthpiece. Sylvia sat down beside her. She played trumpet in the back row. "Last concert, eh, nervous?"

"Yeah. I have four bars on my own, and I really want to pull it off this time. This last concert, I want to be perfect."

"Maggie, you hardly ever miss a note." Sylvia patted her friend on the shoulder. "Your parents coming tonight?"

"No, why would they break with tradition now? I borrowed the car, though, so I can give you a ride home."

"Thanks, but John will drive me."

"You guys going to stay together when school's done?"

"We'll see. He's going to Toronto, and I'm staying here to work, so we'll see. But at least we have the next few months and the prom. You still heading to University of Toronto next?"

"Yeah, it's a great school, and I like Toronto too. Plus it will be a nice change from this little gossip spot."

"Yeah, everyone knows everyone. Well, they think they do. Hey, John's going to Toronto too, so you'll know at least one person." Maggie nodded and smiled, wondering if she would ever run into John in a city as big as Toronto. "You going to prom this year, Maggie?"

"No, I don't think so. But I'm helping with the decorating. I just want to focus on my exams. I need good marks on these."

"You'll do great. You always do. At least come to the final party next weekend. You can't just study all the time. John and are I are picking you up."

Maggie smiled as she put her music on the stand to make sure everything was in order.

"Okay, good, I'll take that as a yes. Good luck tonight."

"You too."

Mr. Stewart walked into the room and started tapping his baton on one of the metal music stands. The room went silent. He gave his standard preparation speech, went through the list of pieces so everyone had their music in order, and then paused. He put his head down for a moment, and the musicians tilted their heads, wondering what was up. Mr. Stewart was always very efficient, not wasting time with unnecessary words.

"I need to say something," he began awkwardly. He didn't know how to speak without the baton. "This will be the last concert for most of you, and I am sorry to see so many of you go. It truly has been an honour to conduct you." He surreptitiously wiped his eye. The band was stunned into silence. Mr. Stewart rarely showed emotion, certainly not like this. As the lead clarinet, Maggie stood up and led the now emotional band onto the stage. The chairs were arranged in four arcing rows, and Maggie made her way to the seat at the front of her section. Clarinets at the front, bassoons and oboes behind, brass third row, and percussion at the back. The lights were bright, the gym was full, and Maggie enjoyed the butterflies in her stomach. It was grand, and she loved it. Mr. Stewart walked to the front and stood on his small, square block. He was short and liked to be able to see his percussion section. Everyone had their eyes on him as he raised his baton, smiled at them all, and winked, which he had never done before. They all smiled back at him. Down went his baton, and the trumpets blared. Their last concert had begun.

When she got home around eleven that night, after the concert and the small celebration at school afterward, she quietly took her shoes off and hung up her jacket. She was hoping to get to her room unnoticed. She closed her eyes slowly and stood still upon hearing her mother's voice.

"Still raining out, Maggie?" her mother called.

"Just a bit, Mom."

"Is the Blender home?" She could hear her dad slur the question in his loud, inebriated voice. She cringed at the unflattering nickname that he used over and over again, regardless of how many times Maggie asked him to stop.

"Well, come and tell us how it went," said her mother. Maggie reluctantly walked into the living room, pipe smoke circling around her dad's head, a half full glass of Scotch in his hand, a half-empty bottle on the table beside him.

"So, how was it?" asked her mom. Her dad didn't once look up from the TV. As he went to place his glass on the side table, he swiped the bottle onto the floor.

"Fucking Christ," he yelled. His wife flinched as he reached to pick up the bottle.

"Don, shush, Tab is asleep."

"Don't you fucking shush me." He pounded the retrieved bottle back onto the table. No one asked about her evening anymore, and Maggie quietly slipped out of the room and upstairs as her parents continued to yell about nothing. University couldn't come fast enough. She just had to get out of this house. She loved Martineville, and she loved Primrose Street. There was always someone with a wave or a smile. The maples gave her a feeling of comfort. She loved their broad trunks, their easy swoosh of leaves and sway of branches. Sometimes she felt caught up in a fabled fantasy, like the maples were whispering stories to her. She couldn't imagine ever living anywhere else. Just not in her parents' house.

There were lots of compliments the next day. The band had made their last concert one to remember. Maggie's playing had been flawless. Even Mr. Stewart had asked her why she wasn't going on to study music. But she knew she would never be good enough to play with a professional orchestra. Still, it was flattering. She realized how much she would miss playing as she handed in her band uniform.

Phil came up beside her. "Handed in the uniform?"

"Yeah, I'll miss it."

"That scratchy stuff? No way. I have something to ease the pain." He pointed to his pocket. Maggie smiled. "At least you're coming to the party next weekend. I'm sure I can convince you there." He leaned into her shoulder as he turned to go. Maggie kept smiling. He made her a bit nervous, but she liked him.

Prom was tomorrow. It had never been a big deal to Maggie, but now that it was the end, she wanted to be part of the last one in some way, and that boiled down to decorations. Daniel Rothwell was president of the student council and in charge of the decorating committee. He wasn't really tall or muscular, but he had a swagger about him. She had fantasized what it would be like to kiss him. He had a defined chest, broad, sexy shoulders, and a tight rear end. Sadly, he always seemed to have a girlfriend, and it hadn't been Maggie. At least she had the satisfaction of working with him at the eleventh hour.

She walked to the student council office, where there was music playing and boxes of balloons, ribbons, and streamers. She saw Daniel at the back of the room and walked over.

"Ah, great, reinforcements have arrived." Daniel walked over and put his arm around Maggie. "Okay, so that box of balloons is yours. And this box of streamers. Come on, I'll show you the plan." They each took a box and started over to the gymnasium. There were already a number of boxes sitting on table in the middle of the room, and the decorating had already begun. Daniel showed Maggie the plan for the balloons and streamers and the table with everything she would need and then said he'd be back. There were drinks and snacks for the workers on the table, and Genesis echoed around the space. It was a party atmosphere. A lot of students had already finished exams. Conversations leaned toward couples that would be at the prom, the last party, where people were going after graduation. Exciting but sad at the same time. Endings. Beginnings. Maggie kept tying balloons together into bunches of four, as directed, with streamers attached to the ends. Another person would come and take her creations and attach them to posts around the gym. As she was bending down to pick up the last four balloons, she felt a hand on her back.

"Almost done? A few of us are heading over to a friend's place in town. He just graduated last year. You know, pizza, beer, want to come?" Maggie always said no. But the alternative was going home.

"Yeah, sure," she said.

"Great, well, we'll put this last one up together, and you can drive over with me." The final decorations were put up, music shut off, tables cleaned up, and Maggie grabbed her stuff.

They stopped to pick up some beer and chips and carried them up the narrow stairwell to the small apartment on the third floor of the complex. The door was opened by a man in his early twenties wearing a pair of jeans. The top button was undone. His hair was most definitely uncombed. There was music in the background and other people of various ages.

"Hey, how's it going. Nabil around?" asked Daniel. The man turned, walked away from the open door and yelled, "Naab." A younger man appeared through the music, wearing a plaid shirt, jeans, and an engaging smile.

"Hey, Nabil, this is Maggie. Maggie, Nabil."

Nabil extended his hand. "Nice to meet you."

"Looks like the place is already hopping."

"Yeah, well, you know, it doesn't take long. But hey, come on in." The music was loud, the conversations were louder, and everyone had some kind of alcohol in their hands. Maggie was beginning to think this had been a huge mistake.

The apartment was sparsely furnished. A small, rectangular table stood at one side of the room, metal legs with a yellowed surface. The chairs around had the same silver legs and yellowed seats, vinyl and slippery to sit on. The galley kitchen was stuffed with beer cases and pizza boxes, chip bags. There was shelf in the corner where a small stereo was playing The Eagles, *Hotel California*. Two orange armchairs in the living room were occupied by girls Maggie recognized from school, smoking and sipping a drink. The couch was probably rescued from a street corner. Dark wood on the arms, stained red velvet covering the cushions, rips down the back. A girl and a guy were on the couch, locked in a long embracing kiss while their hands searched for zippers and buttons. Maggie wasn't sure where to look. Others were standing in various places with various people in animated interaction.

Daniel put his arm around her waist, sensing her discomfort. "Come on, let's have some pizza," and he led her to the kitchen, "and a drink."

"Is there a bathroom?"

"Yeah, just over there," Daniel pointed to the far corner. Maggie took herself across the room, stepping over magazines, peeking into the bedroom with two mattresses on the floor and a British flag covering the window. She closed the door to the bathroom and rested her hands on the vanity. She wasn't sure what she was doing here but decided she'd have one piece of pizza and leave quickly. She could call Sylvia for a ride home. She splashed some water on her face, pinched her cheeks not to look so terrified, and boldly walked back to the kitchen.

Daniel handed her a beer and a slice of pizza, and they sat on the yellow vinyl dining chairs. Nabil came and joined them. He popped off a beer cap and leaned back in his chair.

"Nabil and I did one class together in his last year."

"Yup, and we stayed friends." They clinked their bottles together. "I decided to work in town here before going to college."

"Where do you work?" asked Maggie.

"I work at the grocery store, nothing fancy. I want to do the writing program at one of the colleges, maybe university. I'd like to write for newspapers or magazines."

"Do you do any writing now?"

"Yeah, here and there. I'm trying to do some work for the local paper here, see if I like it. Meantime, I'm just having fun, seeing where things take me, you know. What about you?"

"I'm going to U of T next year to do my B.A., then teacher's college."

"Teaching, eh? Cool. What grade?"

"Probably younger kids. I just think if they don't get a good start, everything will be twice as hard for them later."

"Well, that's true. It was pretty hard for my family when we got here. I could have used some help."

"You needed way more help than she's talking about, my friend," said Daniel.

They laughed together. "Need another beer, Maggie?" asked Nabil as he got up to get more pizza.

She was surprised at how quickly she had finished that beer. "Sure, that'd be great. Thanks."

Nabil came back with more pizza and put a beer in front of Maggie. He pulled some stuff out of his pocket, spread it on the table in front of him, and began rolling a joint. He lit it and began passing it around. When it got to Maggie, she just didn't feel like she could say no. She took a puff and coughed. Nabil laughed. "A little slower, pull it in a little slower." He handed it to her again, and she did what he said. This time she didn't cough, and she felt her body tingle, go a bit limp. It was a different feeling. She took a sip of her beer and wanted another piece of pizza. Suddenly she wasn't feeling so inside out. She got up and went into the kitchen, where the pizza sat on the counter. She began to lift out a piece from the box when she felt Daniel's arms go around her waist, his breath on her neck. She stood very, very still, not sure what to do. But warmth spread through her body.

"I have wanted you for so long," he whispered in her ear. Heat was soaking through her body, a craving she had never felt before.

It was intoxicating. She didn't dare turn around. It was a moment she had fantasized about, and now she was in the middle of it, feeling her heart race, her palms damp, her mouth dry. He slowly began to turn her around to face him. He looked at her. "You're really beautiful," he said. He softly put his lips onto hers and delicately pulled her closer. Her body was on fire, and she knew how easy it would be to say yes, to let her body explode. She had watched him for so long, had fantasized for so long. But thoughts were colliding in her head. She pulled herself back and took a breath..

"What about Annie?"

"We broke up months ago." She wanted him to touch her. She wanted him to take her heat. She wanted more of his mouth. She wanted what her imagination couldn't even articulate. She could hardly breath, and the pulsing in her ears was an ocean. *Not here, not like this, though*, she thought. She knew she didn't want that.

"I think I need to go home, Daniel."

He hesitated and then stepped back. "Sure, I'll take you, no problem."

It was silent in the car as they drove to Maggie's place. Her body was still vibrating with desire. They pulled up to her house, and Daniel looked at her and moved over to kiss her, gently. Softly. She didn't refuse.

"Sorry, Maggie," he said.

"Don't be." She smiled, got out of the car, and went in the front door. She felt Daniel watching her, the engine of his car idling.

The weekend of the party, she took a bit more time than usual to get ready. She was hoping Daniel might be there. She hadn't seen him since that night in Nabil's kitchen. She chose a floral-patterned skirt and pink blouse to match. She used some lipstick and eye shadow and found a pair of sandals with a small heel.

Tabitha looked into her room. "Actually wearing makeup, are you?"

"Get lost, Tabby. Some things are more important than..."

"...than having friends? Okay."

"Is that how you get friends, wearing makeup and spending all your money on clothes? Superficial friends, I might add."

"At least I have friends."

"I have friends. Not suck-ups. Makes me sick how you suck up to Dad too. Can't wait to get out of here." Maggie slammed her door to end the conversation and finished getting ready. She came downstairs, and her dad was in the kitchen, papers all over the table. It was early, so the bottle was only a few drinks empty.

"Hi, honey," he said. "Last party?"

"Yeah, John and Sylvia are picking me up. I won't be home late."

"Last parties you're supposed to come home late. I was always home late from my last parties in high school. Besides, I'll still be sitting here going over these briefs. I have a big case next week, and I don't feel prepared yet. So don't worry, I'll see you when you get home. I'll tell your mom I said no curfew."

"Thanks, Dad."

The doorbell rang. Maggie turned to go.

"Hey, no kiss for your old man?" She went over beside him, and he put his arm around her waist, pulling her close. She bent down and pecked his cheek. He smiled at her, and she half smiled back. Tabitha waltzed into the kitchen and sat down beside her dad, elbows on the table, chin resting on her folded hands.

"Have a great time, honey."

"Yeah, have a great time, honey," mimicked Tabby.

"Thanks, Dad," Maggie said, snarling at her sister.

Maggie heard her dad talking with Tabitha as she left the room. "You'll get your turn soon enough, Sunshine. Don't want my little girl growing up too fast." Maggie just shook her head.

"Hey, you look great." Sylvia touched the sparkling barrette with which Maggie had swept some hair off to the side. "Nice."

"You look great too, but you always look great."

Sylvia smiled. "Thanks, Mag."

"Everything okay?"

"I guess," said Sylvia. "I'm just worried about Mom and Dad. More Mom, I guess. She seems so sad these days that I'm leaving for school. She had a hard time last year when Evan left, but now, I don't know. Makes me feel bad."

"She'll be okay. She has Peter. Your dad's great."

"Yeah, that's the other thing. They aren't the same together these days."

"Sorry, Syl."

"Yeah, I guess stuff happens we don't know about," said Sylvia.

"Sure, stuff happens with *us* they don't know about." They both laugh. "Let's go have some fun."

"Fun parents won't know about!" said Sylvia.

"Deal."

Everyone was at the party. The last hurrah, laughs, tears, kisses, goodbyes. A bittersweet kind of celebration.

"Maggie, you made it. Syl, you look gorgeous, as always."

"That's just sweet, Phil." And she gave him a hug. Some friends were waving to her. "I'll catch you guys later."

"Is this the only party you came to this year, Mag?" said Phil.

"No, I came for a short time to a Christmas party."

"Okay, Mag. Let's make it one to remember!" Phil reached around in his pocket and held up a doobie. Much to his surprise, Maggie reached out for the joint and took a long, slow drag. She handed it back to him and smiled.

"Thanks, Phil."

"Hey no problem, but what is..."

"Hey Maggie," chimed Justin, "this guy bugging ya? Piss off Phil, leave her alone." The two were friends and gave each other a fist bump.

"Just trying to lighten things up, man." Phil laughed and wandered off to another group.

"How are you doing? Excited about leaving this place?" asked Justin.

"Yeah, excited about university, but you know how I love it here."

"Might be nice to get a break from Tab."

"Now that is true!" And they laughed.

"I'm going to Western U in London, do my B.Sc. Then I guess something will come to me. That's as far as I've got. You?"

"U of Toronto, B.A. and then teacher's college."

"Think you'll come back to teach here?"

"Hope so. That's the plan. But I won't be living at home."

"Well, that's no surprise. Want a drink?"

"Sure."

They went over and got a few Cokes with rum. Justin went to talk with other friends, and Maggie went and sat on the back steps. She liked all the lights hanging in the trees. Her favourites were the Chinese paper lanterns, all different colours. The lights reflected through them, creating dancing shapes in between the deeper shadows. She watched all the people she'd spent time in class with, the band, the sports teams. She'd miss it, a lot. Lost in her reverie, she looked up and saw Daniel standing in front of her.

"May I?" he said, pointing to the space on the step beside her.

"Sure."

"You look really pretty tonight. But then you always look pretty."

Maggie smiled. "Thanks. Never knew you were looking."

"More than you know."

"Why didn't you ever say anything?"

"I don't know. Got stuck with Annie, I guess, didn't know how to get out. Plus you always seemed a bit out of my league. In the band, in the library, on sports teams."

"Wow, I never knew. Me and my baggy clothes."

"You're gorgeous under those baggy clothes."

Maggie blushed. "And now? With Annie?"

"We split up because we're going in different directions. And not just different schools. We want different things. I think we always did. Feel I should have figured that out a long time ago. I don't know. It's different with you. Easier." They both sat sipping their drinks, listening to the music, watching the lanterns swing and bob, like moored boats on a quiet evening.

"Hey, listen, I am sorry about the other night," said Daniel.

"Really?"

"Well, I'm sorry if I offended you. I'm not sorry I wanted you."

"Odd timing, when we're all leaving."

"Yeah, I guess. Didn't want to make another bad decision and miss that moment too. I feel I've just missed out being with you."

Maggie didn't know what to say to that. But she knew her heart was beating very, very fast. "Where are you going next year?" she managed.

"Toronto. Engineering."

She smiled at him. "U of T?" she managed to ask.

"Yup."

"Me too."

He reached for her hand, and she let them fold together. It felt nice. Warm. It made her want more. It was like something had been turned on inside her, and she didn't want to turn it off. Daniel leaned over, paused, and then kissed her mouth. This time she didn't stop him. She put her hand up to his cheek, touched his lips with her fingers. She never wanted the kiss to end. The heat travelling down her legs was intense. She wanted to pull him into every cell of her skin. Their faces were inches apart. He whispered, "I never want to lose you Maggie," and he kissed her softly, with rich longing, like a diver reaching for the pearled oyster.

They sat close to each other, gently tracing fingers along arms, legs, cheeks, hair, oblivious to anyone else in the garden.

"When are you leaving for Toronto?" he asked.

"I'm going to look for an apartment next week. I want to work there this summer."

"I'm doing that too." There was a pause. "I want to be with you, Maggie. I always have."

"I want that too." She touched his face.

"I'd better get going, don't want to monopolize you on the last party night," said Daniel. "Can I see you tomorrow?"

"Oh yes, I hope so."

"Can I drive you home when you're ready to go?" She kept holding his hand in reply and smiled.

When she walked in the door that night, her dad was still at the table with all his papers but passed out on top of them, empty bottle on the table, empty glass on the floor. He was snoring. She gingerly walked past him to avoid waking him up and softly closed the door to her room. She heavily leaned her back against the frame, Daniel still on her lips, on her skin. Tingling, resonating, immersed in the feeling as big and as grand as playing Dvořák with the London Philharmonic Orchestra, she crawled under her comforter.

She couldn't wait for tomorrow.

At Nineteen Primrose Street, the roots of the large maple creep underneath the sidewalk. One cement sidewalk slab is cracked in half, arching up. Some of the kids use it as a ramp for their skateboards and bicycles. It really isn't a big deal in the summer, but in winter it is hard to shovel, and ice freezes in awkward spots, making it dangerous to navigate. It has become clear that the tree and the sidewalk are having issues with each other. Many residents feel that it would be a waste of money to adapt the sidewalk but don't want to kill the maple. It is decided there should be a meeting to determine the fate of the tree. Everyone on Primrose Street gathers into the local school's gymnasium one Wednesday evening to discuss the matter. Residents know the drill; they all come in with a plate of something easy to eat and put it on the table: cookies, date square, cheese cubes on toothpicks, chunks of fruit, cases of pop or juice, and tea or coffee. It's a mini potluck of sorts.

The residents like these little gatherings; it's a good excuse to chat and visit. Not everyone shows up, but those who do roam around, pick up a drink and a baked good, chat with neighbours, and find seats together.

Don Carter agrees to chair the meeting. His wife Christine helps organize refreshments. Don has legally represented a lot of residents in Martineville. He knows a lot of people. They think they know him.

"Great you could do this, Don," says Peter. "Doesn't seem like a big deal, but you know how people on Primrose Street are about their maple trees."

"They've been here a long time, no point in just cutting them all down," says Christine, walking back from the kitchen after putting on the kettle for a pot of tea and the coffee pot. Don puts his arm out and catches her hand, pulling her toward him. He puts his arm around her waist and pulls her closer. She smiles stiffly. She can smell the alcohol on his breath.

"Don, seriously, not now," she whispers.

"Always time for hug, my dear. There aren't a lot of people here yet. No rush."

"Look at you two," says Jina as she walks in, "makes me a bit jealous."

"What do you think, Christine?" asks Peter. "To cut or not to cut."

"Oh, fuck, just cut the bastard down. I don't know what all the fuss is about. It's a fucking tree. Look how many others are on the street." Robert talks in a loud voice as he makes his way over to stand beside Don.

"Robert, we know how you feel. Let's hear what other people have to say," says Christine. "Jina?"

"Well, the sidewalk is starting to bulge, I tripped over it the other day. But we can't just cut down all the trees. Maybe replace the sidewalk with those interlocking bricks that move with the frost. Maybe they'd work for trees." Don takes his arm away from Christine, and she doesn't miss her opportunity to slip away.

"Jina," says Don quietly, as if speaking to a child, "that is a very expensive solution and one that will not fly. Maybe best keep that idea to yourself." He winks.

"Thanks, Don, I'll keep that in mind." Jina walks off quickly, thinking the door to the street would be her best bet. But she takes a seat near the back.

"The things that people come up with, I mean, really," says Don.

"What do you fucking expect from a muff diver."

"Who," says Don, "Jina?"

"Oh yeah, haven't you heard?" says Robert.

"I have now. Fuck, that's what we need, some box eaters on the street."

"Don, how does a lesbian build a house?"

"How?"

"All tongue-and-groove, no studs." Robert slaps Don on the back, and they are both laughing, too loudly. Jina is studying her iPhone very closely, trying to settle her rising red anger.

Amiritha walks over and sits in the chair beside Jina. She leans toward her and whispers, "Assholes, forget it."

Jina looks up and smiles. "Thanks." She extends her hand. "I'm Jina."

"Amiritha." Jina puts her phone into her jacket pocket and the two begin to talk, heads close together. The laughter of Robert and Don continues and echoes around the hall.

Jina nudges Amiritha. "Hey, isn't that the guy you were talking to at the wedding?" She nudges her again. Amiritha blushes but follows Jina's eyes. She smiles and waves. Justin catches her wave and smiles back. He says something to Kevin, who sulks off to where the snacks are waiting, and heads over to where Jina and Amiritha are sitting.

"Is this seat taken?"

"No," says Jina, "I think it has your name on it." Amiritha gives Jina's leg a grateful-but-I-don't-want-to-admit-it tap and turns to talk with Justin.

When Mary and Graham walk in, she squeezes his hand a bit tighter upon seeing Robert and Don together, laughing. Graham returns her squeeze. "It's okay, honeybun, you go talk with Maggie and I'll deal with the local talent." He kisses her and heads over. Mary sees Maggie and waves.

"Hey, how is the new bride?" asks Maggie.

"Well, let's just say I never imagined that a piece of cheese could lead to bliss. Gives a whole new meaning to bacterial cultures."

Maggie leans over and gives her friend a hug. "Hey, what are friends for?"

"Is Daniel here tonight?" asks Mary.

"No, he had some work to do. He figured I'd look after things. Plus, he knew my dad would be here."

"Well, that's a challenge for everyone."

"Yeah, especially when Robert shows up too. Seriously, I just don't understand why my mom and Cheryl keep taking their crap. Actually, it really bothers Daniel too. You know, we still get calls from Mom in the middle of the night, in tears. It's the same words over and over."

Charlie comes up behind them and puts his arms over Maggie and Mary's shoulders. His hearing aid doesn't always work too well, making his voice exceptionally loud.

"Miss Maggie Carter and our new Primrose Street bride. What a pleasure."

"It's Maggie Rothwell now, Charlie."

"Eh? What's that dear?"

"Maggie Rothwell," she says a little louder.

"Oh yes, yes." She's never quite sure if Charlie really hears words correctly, but she won't say it twice. He has his pride in large groups. "Mother, look who I found," he says in an overly loud voice to his wife, who looks in his direction. Cora comes over and gives everyone a kiss on the cheek.

"Lovely man, that Graham. You're a lucky girl, Mary," she says. "Almost as lucky as me with my Charlie." And she gives her husband a sparkly smile. He responds by putting his arm around her and pulling her to his side, kissing her cheek.

"Yes, I most certainly am," replies Mary. She looks longingly over at Graham, jesting with the jesters. "If we can be half as happy as you two, we'll count it a success."

A shrill little scream is heard as Nicolas races into the room, followed by Ronald. They race around and end up grabbing onto Cora's legs.

"Grandma, he has my car," says Ronald.

"Does he now. Nicolas, what's in your little hand? Let Grandma Cora have a look now." But Nicolas isn't giving up anything. Sofia walks over, roughly pries the car out of his hand, gives it to Ronald, and picks up the now wailing Nicolas.

"Sorry," she says meekly and hurries away. They all watch her go, not knowing what to say. She is very new to Primrose Street.

Evan and Amanda are getting a drink and a cookie. Maggie walks over to say hi.

"Night off from the hospital for both of you on the same night? I'm sort of wondering what you're doing here."

"Well, it's nice to see everyone, plus we really don't want the maple chopped down, so figured we should show up," says Amanda.

"But then we'll be heading home." Evan winks. They both giggle.

"And Daniel?" asks Amanda.

"Working," says Maggie. "How's Jessica doing?"

"Better. I think her flesh wounds will heal before her heart. But lately she's been talking about applying for a job at the campus in town. That's a good sign. It would be great for her to have a goal like that."

"That is good. I could pick up some applications and information if you like. Should I drop it off at the hospital for you?"

"You know, why don't you take it to her yourself. I think it would mean a lot. Right now it's only her mom that comes to visit."

"I can do that."

"Tabitha has entered," says Evan. They all turn to look, and there she is, fashion model at every turn, her two kids dressed to the nines as well. Dayna follows behind, her kids in tow.

"Hi, Mag, how's it going," offers Tabitha.

"It's good, Tab, you?" asks Maggie.

"There's stress at work, but then Dad's still there to help out."

"So not much has changed, really."

"Jesus, Maggie, let it go already."

Maggie wrinkles her nose at her sister. "Nice pantsuit, by the way."

"Yeah, I just love this material. Hey, Dad's here. I'm going to say hi. See ya, Mag." Maggie looks over to Evan and rolls her eyes, and he just laughs. Everyone on the street is aware of Tabitha's attitude. They were all amazed when she found someone to marry her while at law school. Secretly, they felt a little sorry for him. He never shows up at any get-togethers, leaves that up to his wife, it seems. A conversation with Tabby isn't anyone's first choice. When she glances over in Evan's general direction, he quickly becomes occupied with repositioning a chair. Tabitha waltzes by him. She is concerned with very little but herself, it seems.

"Dad," Tabitha calls, crossing the room. Don lifts his head and puts his arms out.

"My baby girl. Great you came. Where are the kids?" Tabitha walks into his big hug and kisses him on the cheek.

"They're finding food, it seems."

"You look beautiful."

"Thanks, Dad. Hey, there's a case I really need to talk with you about. Coming into the office tomorrow?"

"For you, I sure will. Why don't you find a seat, honey. I have to get this thing rolling soon." He pecks her on the cheek, and Tabitha walks over to where Dayna is sitting. She has a seat saved for her and waves. Dayna is one of the few people who has had a long-standing relationship with Tabitha. They've been friends forever. Dayna sees something in Tabitha no one else does.

Mike rudely walks in front of Tabitha and stops abruptly in front of her.

"Hey Tab, you're looking grrrreat."

"Go fuck yourself, Mike." She pushes him aside and goes to sit with Dayna, not missing a step or turning her head.

"Do you think your brother will ever grow up or move away?" she asks her friend.

"Probably not. God, I wish he'd just go and live somewhere else. It's a pretty big world. Surely he can find another town to terrorize." Mike walks behind their chairs, heading to the snack table.

"Who's the new girl, Mike?" asks Dayna.

"None of your biz, sis."

Mike continues over, grabs a date square, and begins talking with Sofia. He's leaning in as he talks, but she leans away, turning her head to one side. He keeps trying to find her eyes. There is an aggressive quality to his manner. He slips his arm around her waist, like he's done it many times before. She visibly tenses but doesn't resist. He guides her over to a couple of chairs, and they sit down. When his arm isn't around her waist, it's around her shoulder. Nicolas comes and climbs on the chair beside Sofia, eyeing Mike as he grabs possessively at his mom.

Ruth is wandering around with a Coke in her hand. She looks a little lost. She has always looked rather lost since Jessica had her meltdown. Rebecca goes over and talks to her.

"How are you doing these days, Ruth?" she asks.

"Some days are better than others for sure. It's really hard going to see Jessica in the hospital. Some days she doesn't even know me."

"She's on a lot of meds, Ruth. Don't expect too much, too fast."

"Yeah, I know, that's what I keep telling myself."

"She'll be okay, she really will."

"Yeah. Then she comes home. I'm not sure how to handle that."

"One thing at a time. Let her get better first. Hey, maybe we should get lunch sometime."

"I don't know. Oh God, look who decided to show up." They both turn to see Susan and Joe awkwardly move into the room. "I'd like to give them a piece of my mind."

"Ruth, that's not going to help anything. Come on, I'll get you a tea and we'll sit down." Rebecca guides Ruth to a chair at the far side of the room and goes to get a couple of teas. She watches Phil's parents out of the corner of her eye as she makes her way to the teapot.

"Don, why don't we get started?" says Peter, noticing tension rising in the room. "We all have other things to do tonight."

"Sure, okay, Peter." Don walks to the front, and Robert leans against a wall at the back. Graham goes over and sits beside Mary, taking her hand.

Don gives an overview of the situation, and people start to give their two cents worth. Others stay quiet and listen. It becomes clear that no one wants to cut down the tree, but no one wants to be injured tripping over a heaving sidewalk either, especially in the winter. Amanda and Evan make it clear they don't want to see anyone from Primrose Street in their ER as a result of the cracked sidewalk.

And so it is decided that part of the root system will be pared away. Everyone will donate some money toward the cost of having this done professionally.

"Seems like a fucking waste of money to me," grumbles Robert. "Just let me get my chainsaw out. That will solve the problem in an hour." There is a collective sigh and a shaking of heads. A few other issues are raised, like the speed limit on the street and a commitment to shovelling sidewalks better in the winter. As the meeting comes to a close, everyone gets up and mingles. They take their time finishing off the snacks, sipping on sodas. Some people exit quickly, not wanting a scene. The kids run around, using people as pylons. Seems that almost everyone really does hope the tree lives. Especially Phil's mom. Susan doesn't come out to many gatherings, and her husband attends even fewer. They keep to themselves.

The tree in question sits in front of their house. She remembers how Phil gazed at that tree from his bedroom window his whole life. What she doesn't know is how much strength and comfort he took from that maple when the world seemed especially unkind and unfeeling and intolerant. The tree helped him through elementary and then high school. Sometimes he would crawl up into her branches to inhale his marijuana in peace. Weed and the tree preserved his sanity. All through high school he had been the clown, the fun Phil. No one but the tree knew his agony.

NINETEEN PRIMROSE STREET:
PHIL

P hil was ten years old. His dad had picked him up from hockey practice. He dropped his bag in the foyer when he got home and went into the kitchen for his after-hockey snack. His mom always had something special that he liked ready. Some days it was celery with Cheez Whiz. Maybe crackers and cream cheese. On special days, when the team won a game, she'd have chocolate cake and ice cream. Today it was peanut butter cookies and milk. He sat on the stool, waiting and chatting with her. He looked forward to telling her about his day. It was the only time his brothers and sisters were somewhere else.

"How was practice today, honey?"

"I like the coach this year. He's cool."

"How about the other players? Are they better this year? Think you have a chance at winning some games?"

"Yeah, I think so. I really like this one guy, Tony. He's a forward."

"Think he could be a good friend?"

"I hope so. My heart gets all tense when I see him, and my stomach feels like it has butterflies in it." His mother's hand froze, hovering in midair while struggling to keep holding the plate.

"What did you say, Phil?"

"That I really like Tony. Someday, I'd like to kiss him." The dish smashed on the floor as his mother lunged at Phil, grabbed him by the shirt, pulled him off the chair, and dragged him up to the bathroom. Phil had no idea what was happening, but he was scared. He had never seen his mother like this. She was the peacemaker in the house, always so soft-spoken. Now she was breathing through her teeth and seemed to have superhuman strength. She wedged him into the sink with her thigh, turned on the tap, and proceeded to wash his mouth out with a bar of soap, yelling at him the whole time. No, screeching.

"Never, never do I want to hear those filthy words come out of your mouth again." Phil was gagging now on the soap going down his throat, and tears were welling up. "Never, Phil, never." She threw the bar of soap in the sink and began washing her hands over and over again. Phil sank to the floor, sobbing. His mother stood over him. His father and siblings hovered outside the bathroom door.

"I can't even look at you. Go to your room. No dinner for you tonight." She walked out, slamming the door. He heard her footsteps going down the stairs and the muted whispers of his father trying to calm her down.

He made it through the next few years and all the sports teams, always telling his mother exactly what she wanted to hear, and everyone else, for that matter. When he found marijuana, he found relief, calm. He smoked a lot. It made it easier to walk around in the costume he felt forced to wear. While high, he really couldn't give a shit. He took girls to proms or the movies, mostly when his mother set him up with a friend of the family's daughter. He knew the moves, knew what he was supposed to do, and he did. But he never went further than a feel and a kiss. He couldn't, he just couldn't. No one knew, not a soul.

He hated sports. But he loved the high school band. Music was his other marijuana. It was the only place that he was real. And everyone appreciated his talent and passion. He never froze when he had a solo. He played at least four instruments but really loved the French horn. He knew he would go on to play in an orchestra, somewhere, someday. But not near Martineville. He never wanted to see Martineville again. He wanted to go to the other side of the country. He applied for the music program at the University of British Columbia, was accepted on a scholarship, and left after his last exam. He packed a small bag, said his goodbyes, and gave the appropriate number of hugs. His mother cried and said she would miss him. He did not believe she would. He got on the bus without looking back.

British Columbia was a different world for Phil. Big, bold, beautiful. Caution could be stretched, like someone lurching off a cliff on the end of a bungie line, knowing you'd just bounce back. He began to explore himself without the help of the thin, hand-rolled joint tucked inside his pocket all the time.

It was fresh and clear being able to watch another man and adore him without the protection of a mask. He came to realize that there were many who felt as he did. He had never felt that back home. Never safe.

He was excited about the possibilities as he took his one bag into his room in residence. He liked being the small fish in the big pond. He was excited about exploring other brass instruments in the music program and about exploring Vancouver. The huge, white-capped mountains stood proudly in the distance, the ocean sparkling at their feet. He was awestruck.

The campus was large, and he needed to follow his map to find his first class. He stood in the middle of a walkway, trying to make sense of the directions on the map in his hands, and didn't notice someone was standing beside him.

"Hello?"

Phil looked up.

"Need some help? These maps aren't very helpful. Where are you heading?"

Phil couldn't feel his heartbeat, but he could hear it booming in his ears. He had never seen any man as beautiful as the one standing beside him now. He swallowed so he could answer and not appear a total buffoon.

"Music hall. I'm looking for the music hall."

"Okay, well I'm not going there myself, but I am going to science lab just next door. I'll show you the way."

"Great, that would be great. Thanks." Phil hoped his voice didn't sound squeaky, but he really couldn't trust anything about himself right now. It was all completely new. He felt foreign in his own body.

"First year?"

"Yeah."

"Where are you from?"

"A midsized town in Ontario. You?"

"Hometown boy. And here we are. That's the music hall there, and I'm over there in the claustrophobic science lab. Grad work involves a lot of navel-gazing. Hey, good luck, man."

Phil stood there for a moment. His breath was hard to find. He hadn't even asked the guy's name. But it was quite an introduction to the music hall. He opened the door and walked in... to wonder. He was gobsmacked at the size of the place. Acoustics would be sick. Just sick. People were getting music stands lined up, and instrument cases were opening all over the space. He walked over and signed in, picking up his French horn. He took a seat in the brass row beside a young woman with shoulder-length brown hair and a handful of trumpet.

"Hey, I'm Phil."

"Tina, nice to meet you. You scared?"

"Yeah. Can't lie. This is a pretty intense way to start... playing together first week. But I guess we'll see what we've got pretty fast, right?"

"I guess."

They arranged the music they were handed, and slowly the orchestra pieced itself together and the professor/conductor stood in front of them.

"Greetings, newcomers. We'll get to formal introductions and course expectations a little later. Right now, I'm throwing you all together with a piece of music in front of you. We are going to play cold, ladies and gentleman. Welcome. Instruments ready, please..." He waved his baton, and magic happened. It was like they had always played together. Smooth, textured, vibrant. Phil felt chills down his spine. He had never encountered anything like it before. The brass was striking, the woodwinds clear and clean, percussion vibrated with the rhythms of the room.

They played a few more pieces and then had the pleasure of being picked apart by their maestro. It was a bit of a downer, but to be expected. Still, they were good. If that meant they could get better, that was exciting. Course expectations were explained, theory classes were outlined. They were also responsible for an English and a history class, and one science lab for dummies, as it was called, to fulfill requirements of their degree.

Phil walked out with a headful and an armful of material he would have to go over. He walked over to the bookstore to pick up some of the required reading texts for his liberal arts options. The science lab didn't require any texts, just hands-on work. Many people opted for that course because of that. A group suggested going over to the University Centre for a pint.

The pub was full of noise and laughter and students. Crazy cool. They sat around a large round table and ordered a jug of beer. Glasses appeared, people started drinking, and Phil recognized a familiar fragrance circling the room.

Tina had her nose in the air, sniffing. "Oh yeah, wish I could have a drag, just a small one."

"Really?" said Phil.

"Yes, you?" And in response, Phil pulled out his little treat resting in his pocket.

"Cool," said Tina, and the rest of the table smiled as Phil passed the joint around.

Introductions became easier, conversations flowed, and a second jug appeared on the table. Phil watched a new group come into the pub and sit across the room. The guy that had helped him find the music hall sat down. Phil felt his stomach lurch. The guy looked right at him and made his way across the room.

"Hey, man, nice to see you. How was first class?'

"Great, just great."

"Listen, I forgot to give you my name this morning. It's Antonio."

"Phil." And they shook hands.

"Hey, we're getting a pizza down in the lounge around seven thirty, do you want to join us?"

"Great, love to."

"Okay, see you there?"

Phil got to know some of the other people in his class and helped them finish off the last jug of beer. He couldn't get his mind off Antonio. There was just something about him. But he needed to get his stuff together, so he headed over to his dorm room to go over his schedule, organize his papers, and have a shower.

He lay on his bed reading one of the books on the English reading list, *Vanity Fair*. Wouldn't have been his first choice, but he struggled to the end of the first chapter and noticed it was already seven, so he got dressed and headed over to the lounge.

There were a lot of people milling about, reading, socializing. He stood searching the room when he felt a presence behind him. He turned.

"You have got to stop doing that," he said to Antonio.

"Yeah, sorry, I just seem to find you in a daydream each time I see you. Come on over and sit." He led the way over to a group of leather couches.

"We can order the pizza any time you want. Hungry?"

"Don't you want to wait for the others?"

"Actually, I have to be honest," and he placed a hand on Phil's knee, "I just wanted to get to know *you* a bit better."

Phil felt a pressure across his chest. *Be cool, be cool*, he kept saying to himself. For years he had pretended to be attracted to girls and looked away from boys. And here was this gorgeous man coming on to him in public. He had no words. No thoughts. He just responded. He instinctively put his hand on top of Antonio's. He had wanted to know what it was like to feel this way his whole life. To touch another man, and not on a sports team. He wanted to get out of the tight, ill-fitting costume he had been put into years ago. He sat there with nothing to say.

"Come on," Antonio said, "let's get out of here."

They walked the paths around the university and talked and talked. Antonio shared the charade he had lived with in a big Catholic family. Phil told him everything, everything he had never told anyone. And Antonio listened. Finally, when his monologue ended, they stopped in the shadow of a large tree and faced each other. Antonio put his arms around Phil, pulled him close, and kissed him. Kissed him hard on the lips, and Phil's hands slipped down to Antonio's lower back and then cradled his ass, holding them there, never wanting them to move and let himself kiss back. Antonio pushed his body tighter against Phil. He felt for his tongue, felt for his lips. And they stood in that exact embrace, not moving for what seemed like hours.

And so the semester began. The orchestra continued to improve. Phil got through *Vanity Fair*. He didn't need the map any more. Antonio helped him with his lab class. They spent a lot of time in the lab. Antonio was usually there finishing experiments late into the night, and Phil would study and watch him and wait. He didn't want to say it out loud, but he loved Antonio; he knew it. He felt different. Like he could touch the moon. Like he could swim across the ocean. Wrestle sharks. Antonio inspired him, changed him, helped him find out who he was, who he could be. Even his music took on a different tone. They did have to be cautious, though. Phil often wondered what people thought. Did they think he liked to be that different? That he wanted a life that had to be lived in secret? That the one he loved had to be hidden in the shadows? That he enjoyed hearing the cruel comments made at pub tables about gays, and that if he didn't laugh with them, he'd be pounded black and blue? Did they really think it was a choice? It was who he was, plain and simple. No choice. Another colour on the artist's palette. But most still wanted to wipe that colour off the board. They saw them as pedophiles, sexual deviants, perverts. But the way he felt about Antonio couldn't be further from the truth. He wouldn't dream of thinking something demented about a man in a heterosexual relationship. He wondered how long it would be until he was afforded that same respect.

Antonio didn't have a lab that night and had asked if Phil wanted to meet down by the water, walk a bit, and then get a bite. He said he had something he needed to tell him.

Phil saw him standing by the ocean's edge as the waves slowly fingered their way onto the sand. The ocean was quiet today. He walked up and stood quietly beside him. Antonio put his arm around Phil's shoulders. They stood like that for some time, quietly feeling the heat of each other's bodies, the pulse of the ocean, the movement of the sand. Gulls flew overhead, calling for food. The huge trees lining Stanley Park hovered, watching.

"I'm getting married in six months," said Antonio. Neither moved. Only the sand slipped away under around their feet. Phil didn't know what to say. Antonio turned to look at him.

"Phil, you know that I love you." He had said out loud what Phil had been too scared to say.

"Then why? What is happening?" Phil thought he was going to be sick all over his shoes.

Antonio turned to look him in the face. "Listen, I'm just going to say this straight out. Okay? Jessica is a grad student as well. We've been living together for over a year. It was a couple of years ago, and things weren't as easy, you know, for guys like us. I mean, you know, the act, everything. And sometimes about getting beaten up. And I was tired of it, really tired of it. That's when I met Jessica. She's beautiful, smart, funny. And suddenly, I was accepted. As long as I was dating this beautiful, successful woman, it didn't seem to matter what I did. I didn't flaunt anything in public or stuff like that, but it was like the pressure was taken off me. She was my cover. I mean she's great, don't get me wrong, but she's not you. But I can never have you like that. So what I want to ask is, can you still be with me knowing this? And if you can, then I want us all to be friends."

"Does she know, you know, that you're gay, that you love me?"

"No. On both counts. No." He looked down. "I'm not proud of this, Phil. It all makes me sick. I mean, they kill guys like us in Russia and Egypt and Africa. Kill us for who we are. Insane. But it is what it is, so I'm playing the game so I get something I want. You. And I don't want either one of us in the hospital or worse. We need a cover. Plain and simple." He reached out his hand. Phil took it. Held it.

"So she really doesn't know?"

"No, not a thing. And it has to stay like that. I've told her I met this cool guy, though. He couldn't read the university map. She got a kick out of that, said she wanted to meet you. So will you come to dinner on Saturday?"

Phil stood there. He knew what it was like to pretend. He never imagined it would come to this, and that it was really so bad.

"Yes, I'll come. What happens to us, though?"

"Nothing. We just stay friends in public and around Jessica and have our real relationship whenever we can in private. Can you live with that?"

"I don't have much choice." He looked down. "What about Jessica?"

"Yeah, I know. I do love her, you know, in a way I can't explain. I'll care for her, but I can't see any other way."

"Yeah." Phil paused. "I love you too, Antonio."

Antonio put his finger under Phil's chin and lifted it. He looked him in the eye and then kissed him, gently, with longing. "Okay, 7:00 p.m. Saturday?"

"Okay."

Phil thought it would have been different on the west coast, and it was, but not entirely. He didn't feel great about the whole arrangement. Not a choice at all. He still felt a bit sick.

Saturday came. He found the address that Antonio had written down for him. He carried a bottle of red wine under his arm and his signature smoke in his pocket... just in case. He wasn't sure what the "in case" really was but thought it was a good idea to have it along for the ride. He had already taken a puff to calm his nerves that were leaping under his skin. He wasn't sure how he was going to pull this off, but he knew what it was to be something he wasn't. Years of practice. He pulled on the tight, ill-fitting costume once again. He knocked, tentatively.

The door was opened by a young woman with light brown hair flowing around her shoulders and an open smile. They stood staring at each other.

"Oh my god," she screamed. "Oh my god, I can't believe it, I had no idea. Phil, what the fuck. Welcome, welcome." And she jumped across the threshold to pull Phil into a bear hug. Phil extended the bottle of wine.

"Awesome, thank you, come on in. Antoooniiio. Phil's here," she called out. Antonio came around the corner. "Tony, you didn't tell me it was *this* Phil. Don't you know? We went to high school together and played under the chestnut tree. Remember, Phil? Wow, such a long time ago. Like another life." It was all Antonio could do not to let his chin actually hit the floor. Phil was in a state of shock. He was having trouble getting through the door.

"What?"

"It's true," said Phil. "Martineville High. And before that, we lived close to each other on Primrose Street. We had a pretty successful lemonade stand one year, I think. But we didn't see as much of each other during high school. Me music, she science. But yep, same town. Go figure." Phil wanted a large hole to present itself that he could just slip quietly into it, forever.

"Oh my god. I just can't believe it," she kept repeating. "Phil. And you look so great. I'm sure the girls out here are swooning over you. If you don't have someone special yet, I have a couple of friends you need to meet. Fuck, the sauce," and she flew into the small kitchen.

Phil turned around. He just stared blankly at Antonio, who had paled significantly. "Hey, man." He went to shake Antonio's hand, to make a show for Jessica, lingering for as long as possible. Antonio pulled away and went into the kitchen, putting his arm around Jessica's waist.

"Smells good, honey. Shall I open the bottle of wine?"

"Great, and pour everyone a glass." Antonio popped the cork and poured. He handed Jessica a glass first then took one over to Phil.

"Hmm, great wine, Phil. Thanks. Such a treat. I really hate beer, but it's cheap."

"I also brought something else, if that's okay. If not, it will just stay in my pocket."

Jessica spun around. "Nooooo, seriously, you brought some good stuff. I should have known. You always had the good stuff in high school. Get it out. It will definitely improve the dinner. I'm not the best cook."

Phil went to his jacket and pulled out his joint. He lit it and passed it around. Everyone took a long drag.

"Oh yeah, that's better. Antonio, we really need to get some of this stuff. Oh, that's nice. Okay, sauce, here I come. Why don't you guys set the table and then just yak in there. I'm pretty happy here with my wine and my buzz right now."

Phil and Antonio set the table, talking about classes, campus, carrying on a different conversation with their eyes but being cautious and wary. Jessica brought in a large blue bowl filled with pasta and sauce. She put it in the centre of the tiny table.

"Can you grab the parmesan, honey? Okay, let's eat."

It was a nice evening. They ate, drank, caught up, talked, listened to music, and finally Phil said he would call it a night. She hugged him on the way out.

"Great to see you again, maybe for the first time. I see why Antonio has taken a shine to you. Great to have good friends, hope we'll see more of you." Antonio came over and put his arm around Jessica's waist.

"Yeah, man. Don't be a stranger. See you on campus." And the door closed. Phil stood in the hall. Insane. Crazy. But now that he knew what Antonio was doing, he had discovered so many others doing the same thing. Poison, really. Poison for everyone. But this poison he would drink. He knew it would never get better than this for him. But Jessica. It was bad enough when she was a stranger, but Jessica from Martineville, seriously, what were the chances. *Fuck*. He felt sick again. He pulled out the smoke and finished it on the way home.

As the months passed, Jessica, Antonio, and Phil spent more and more time together. They rented a chalet at Whistler for weekends and went skiing. They had picnics in the park. They studied together. And Antonio would meet Phil in shadowed places and express all that had been missing during the days and nights. They lived two lives. They collected quickly, the lies, like snowflakes in the mountains piling into drifts around their feet, reaching up to block the light from their windows. Phil thought Jessica was wonderful. Antonio and Phil convinced themselves that as long as they were careful, she would never know and no one would get hurt. Win/win for everyone.

The wedding day approached. Antonio asked Phil to be his best man. He accepted. Jessica was thrilled. The wedding was down by the ocean. Tents had been set up, and it proved to be a glorious day. The wedding was scheduled for 2:00 p.m., with dinner and dancing to follow. Jessica would stay with friends the night before and Antonio with different friends. Tradition said this was the way things were done. It added to the mystery, apparently. Antonio stayed with Phil in a hotel room.

"To me, this is our wedding night, Phil. For me, this is really us getting married. It is you I love, and I need you in my life always."

Things were so confusing, but when Antonio said this, all the things Phil had wanted to say about Jessica and him, Jessica and Antonio, the whole situation, flew out the window on the wings of nightingales. They were in each other's arms, kissing like they had never done before. All the weeks and days and months of pretending slipped to the floor with their clothes, and they clung to each other and pulled closer and loved each other like neither thought possible. They touched and kissed and pleasured each other over and over again, interspersed with drags from Phil's offering. By morning, they hadn't slept and just stayed in each other's arms, reluctant to leave, terrified of what was to come. They dressed each other, stealing kisses along the way, and hailed a cab together.

Antonio was late. He ran to the gathering, saw Jessica, and waved. She could see him puffing. But he was there, which was all that mattered. She waved to Phil. He smiled and waved back. Everyone stood in their places, statues in an artist's carving, fixed in their respective roles. They vowed, they kissed, they held hands as everyone clapped and cheered the new Mr. and Mrs.

Phil danced with Jessica. She made him promise to always be there. He did.

Antonio and Jessica moved to Seattle down the coast, where there were better jobs in their fields. Phil had a few more years at UBC. They stayed in touch. They were only a two-hour bus ride away. Antonio would take business trips to Vancouver and stay with Phil. Their love never wavered. Phil would spend Christmases with them in Seattle. Sometimes, Phil would secretly join Antonio on a business trip.

Their second anniversary was coming up. They were planning a trip to the beaches of Mexico. Antonio sent the info to Phil. He asked if he was able to come and stay in the hotel down the beach from where he would be staying with Jessica. They could make time to be together, like an anniversary trip of their own.

Phil agreed. He was doing his masters degree in music and would be auditioning for the Vancouver Symphony. He needed a vacation anyway. And secrets were the way of his life. It was just like brushing his teeth.

The maple's leaves, hanging delicately from their branches, like to dance just outside windows. The veins on the leaves are pronounced in the thick afternoon light, as if the rays have been compressed and the brightness implodes. There is an electricity pulsing through the red lines pressed onto the leaf face. They reflect the thoughts of those caught up in the dance. Maggie reaches out to touch the window pane in front of her, as if connecting with the five points of the leaf, wanting to pull that iridescence into her being for inspiration.

She loves the little house she and Daniel bought in Martineville. She had so hoped to find a place on Primrose Street, but on reflection, she didn't think she could be THAT close to her parents. Turned out they were right between both families. There are some beautiful maples on their lot, which makes her happy, and so does Daniel. He is so supportive and not just about what she does, but who she is. Since being with Daniel, Maggie enjoys her food more, and she is starting to wear clothes that really fit her. She feels good about her body for the first time. If Rita could only see her now, she sometimes thinks to herself.

She was so lucky to get the teaching position when it came up at the local school. Daniel knew how important it was to her, so he relocated his job so they could live in Martineville. He was happy to come home too. Maggie is very dedicated to her job. She cares about her students deeply.

Ronald is a challenging student for her. He is always polite and helpful but shrinks when presented with any academic task. The leaves catching her gaze blur as she imagines Ronald at his desk. He is sullen and confused. She knows his angst is real and not just a charade to get out of work, like a lot of other boys in the class. When they work with visuals on an iPad or the SMART board, he is quick to answer and participate. But when he is presented with a passage to read, he noticeably shrinks in his seat, asks to go to the bathroom, and pales. His test scores are low, and yet she knows he is a bright boy. At this juncture, his academic path will not support his inquisitive mind, unless she can find a way to inspire him, to find the tool that will help him want to reach into words and pull out their meaning.

Maggie has searched and read and investigated, tried different approaches, but nothing has brought Ronald closer to being happy at school. And the teasing is getting worse. Going to the special education teacher, Mrs. Cole, doesn't seem to be helping him. It makes him stand out even more. Other students can be vicious, like integrating a new animal into a herd. Maggie watched it happen at her uncle's farm time and again when he'd put a new horse into the pasture. The initiate would be let into the field, and instead of the residents welcoming the newcomer, they would chase the poor thing into a frothy sweat. They would have run that horse to death if her uncle hadn't intervened and taken him out. It would sometimes take days for integration and acceptance to happen. And if the horse was white, the games would be more vicious and last longer. A white horse stands out in the wild, makes the herd more vulnerable to attacks, and so the white horse is danger. Ronald seems to suffer as would a white horse. He is seen as the one who will bring problems to the others. Maggie wants to find a way for him to be in the field safely.

SEVEN PRIMROSE STREET: RONALD

Ronald Burke lay on his bed, watching the sunlight play across his ceiling. It was Saturday, which meant he didn't have to walk to the end of Primrose Street and wait for the school bus. Ronald hated the school bus. He hated school too. He especially hated walking down the hall with Mrs. Cole, who made him work all by himself in her small room. He never got to use the same books as the other kids. They would tease him when he came back from working with Mrs. Cole. "Grade four is too hard for Ronald. Maybe he should go back to kindergarten." Everyone would laugh and point. Ronald hated school.

But Ronald loved his house and the huge backyard. He loved the tall maple tree that stood in the yard just outside his bedroom window. He called her Maple, and she was his friend. Grandma Cora had big maples outside her house. She loved her maples as much as Ronald loved his. He could tell Grandma Cora about his tree. She understood when he told her. The leaves would waltz into his window on morning breezes, coaxing him to come and play, teasing him with floating leaves that dipped down to tickle his cheek. *Come, try to climb into my tip-top branches*, she would whisper. He'd imagine himself tucked high amongst the leaves, closer to the stars and far, far away from the school bus. He loved to look at the stars at night through his bedroom window. Grandma Cora had given him a small telescope one Christmas, and he peered at the stars.

Ronald slid out of bed the next morning, waiting until his feet touched the floor, stuffed his legs into crumpled pants, crunched his feet into waiting shoes, ran into the kitchen, and hoped he was big enough to reach the cookie jar on the counter without standing on a chair. He reached and stretched, but it was just out of his grasp. He went to get the chair. His tree was waiting for him. He had to find a way to the top. He just had to.

In spring, he would lie underneath her large limbs, waiting for buds to burst into cool, green leaves, studying the angles in the branches overhead. For a small boy, he had big pockets of patience.

In summer, he would sprawl in her cool shade, munching on watermelon slices, looking up and making plans for how he would one day reach the top. Maybe he could nail wooden boards onto the trunk to help him climb up. Nails. It would make it easier to climb, but he didn't want to hurt Maple. As he lay in the soft grass, gazing up, he could almost see himself moving up the bark, pausing for breath, climbing higher and higher until her canopy was reached. He would make it up there one day, he was now determined.

In autumn, he would rake and rerake the colourful leaves, making piles of fun over and over again. When he got tired of raking and jumping, he'd lie back and watch as Maple shook herself free of summer, preparing for her winter clothes.

In winter, she looked cold and hard and slippery and taller than ever. The tree was now bare, but Ronald began to wear more and more layers of clothing as snowflakes fell. He made elaborate snow forts around her trunk, and Maple would sprinkle him with snowflakes and ice crystals. He laughed and threw snowballs back, decorating her bark with splats of snow frosting.

Winter was long and cold. It was sometimes still dark as he stood at the end of the lane, waiting for the school bus. Mrs. Cole had more work each week. If he didn't always get teased, he would rather have stayed in the classroom with Mrs. Rothwell. She was the only good thing about going to school. She'd give out suckers if the class tried hard. She always smiled when he did his best, and it made him want to do better. He didn't know why he had to go to Mrs. Cole's room. He hated her and her tests and fake laugh. The other students, who got to stay with Mrs. Rothwell, always seemed to be having fun. Ronald wondered if winter would ever end.

Then one April morning, as he started to get out of bed, his feet touched the floor before sliding down! Maple's spring leaves, fandango'ing through the open window, tickled him around his ears. Right then he knew he was big enough to climb the tree... and to reach the cookie jar.

It wasn't an easy climb, but his arms were stronger now; so were his legs and his resolve. It was really hard getting up the trunk, since he kept slipping and sliding, so he went to get his dad's ladder and propped it up against the tree... one last push and he could reach the first big branch. He looked up and kept going. He got caught up on branches, bloodied his elbow and cut his lip, but he pressed on, grabbing, grasping, and scraping all the way up into those tip-top branches.

He had done it. *HURRAY!!! HURRAY!!!* He settled into one of the broad and comforting limbs, feeling like a king, reaching into his pocket to pull out a cookie he'd taken from the jar in celebration. A strong breeze moved the branches back and forth, and he felt like his friend was giving him a cheer.

It was the tallest tree in the world, he was sure of that. He could see over the roofs of neighbouring houses. As he squinted, he could see even farther. He could see all the way over to Main Street and Graham's shop. He loved going there; Graham always had some treat for him. Sitting up in his tree, he could see Grandma Cora's house.

As he proudly perched, gazing into the distance, he leaned his head back, looked up, and got an idea. This was much higher than his bedroom window. Stargazing would be so much better from here... maybe he could see Venus or Mars from the tree — or maybe Santa and his reindeer! They would have more lights than just Rudolph's nose; there would be eight bright night-lights. They would be the brightest lights in the sky on Christmas Eve. *YES!!!!*

Now Ronald had a real project, better than anything at school: to see Santa's sleigh ride on Christmas Eve.

That night, after dinner, Ronald asked his dad how to make a rope ladder. He had decided this was better than nails or a propped-up ladder. His dad asked why he needed a rope ladder, and Ronald told him his plan. He was so excited, pointing up to the branches, showing his dad the cut on his lip like it was a badge of honour. "I don't really know how I'm going to do it yet, Dad, but I really want to try."

His dad was happy to see Ronald so excited. They went to the workshop and started to find bits and pieces that could be made into a ladder. Mr. Burke was surprised at how quickly Ronald learned to use a measuring tape and how accurate he was at drawing his lines and marks. He always seemed to struggle with every subject at school. Maggie Rothwell was a good teacher. She seemed to understand Ronald and had given him a lot of help. He made a note to tell her about this project of Ronald's.

That weekend they worked together to get the rope ladder in place. It was quite a job bringing his small telescope up the tree into the highest branches. When he dropped it, pieces would chip off as it crashed into branches on the way down. A few times Ronald almost fell out of the tree trying to catch it. He needed a plan.

Ronald started to make drawings of a platform in the tree and a place where a box could go to hold his equipment. He showed his dad, who looked at him with great surprise. That evening Ronald learned to use other tools.

That summer, he and his dad worked together and began to build his platform. Ronald used the power saw, and nails and a hammer. His dad watched with pride how careful Ronald was and how well he followed instructions. Ronald had found a book at the library about making treehouses. He showed it to his dad and read him a part about how they got big pieces into the tree. Mr. Burke was amazed at how well Ronald could read. He was also impressed with Ronald's idea for moving the finished platform. They created a pulley system to get the finished product up into its place between two big branches, halfway up.

When they finished, they sat under the tree together, and Ronald eagerly showed his dad the books about stars and telescopes. His mother brought them a tray with two lemonades and some watermelon slices.

"Thanks, Mom."

Mrs. Burke leaned down and gave Ronald a kiss on the head. His dad lifted his glass of lemonade toward Ronald. "Cheers, my boy. To your project and a job well done." Ronald lifted his own glass and clinked it with his dad's. They each took a long drink and smiled at each other.

After that, Ronald spent all his time up in the tree. Only lightning storms could keep him away, and that was only because his mother told him it could be dangerous and wouldn't let him climb up.

And then autumn leaves began making space for the cold winds of a Canadian winter, and climbing became tricky at best. That winter, unless there was a rip-roaring snowstorm with winds so strong Ronald might get blown right out of that tree, or a frostbite warning, each day after school he'd quickly do his homework, pack his cookies and hot chocolate into his knapsack, and make his way up the tree. In winter he'd climb and watch and plan. He was getting very familiar with the stars in the northern sky. He had scraps of paper all over his room with different pulley systems, waterproof box options, ladders, and different routes to the top, as well as books about telescopes and constellations.

That Christmas Eve he bunked down in the topmost branches and waited to see the magical sleigh and eight reindeer. His little telescope was not very strong, but Ronald was curious about stars he saw in patterns and how some were brighter than others. Those were the coldest days in the tree, when he needed extra hot chocolate inside his tummy and an extra sweater inside his coat.

But on that special night of peace, Ronald noticed more and more tiny night stars in the sky and felt a tingling kind of warmth deep inside. He peered through his tiny telescope for eight little lights in a row, but he couldn't find them. *It's a big sky*, he thought, *I'll just have to keep looking.*

When he woke next morning, Christmas Day, there was a brand new big, waterproof telescope under the tree. He ran to hug his mom and dad. "This is awesome, just awesome!"

After the holidays, when he went back to school, he asked Mrs. Rothwell if they had any books on stars.

"Sure, Ronald, they have quite a few in the library, and we can find some websites too. Your dad was telling me about your tree project. It sounds very exciting."

"It is," he said. "Can we find those books now?" Maggie smiled and led Ronald to the library. There were at least five books that would suit, and Ronald was very happy. On one of the really cold days, too cold to go outside for recess, he sat at his desk, gazing at one of the astronomy books.

Another boy, Sherwin, stood beside him and said nastily, "Twinkle twinkle little Ronald," but before he could start to laugh, Ronald spoke without looking up.

"That star is Venus, Sherwin. It's not called Ronald. And it's not little, it's huge."

Sherwin stood very still and was very quiet. For the first time, he had no answer.

Ronald's project became more sophisticated the next summer. With his building skills and help from his dad, he had now put a waterproof box onto the platform so he wouldn't have to lug his telescope up and down the tree each time. This was an expensive telescope, and he didn't want to risk having it crash down the tree. He also had a little space inside his box for a thermos, his cookie jar, and a few books about stars.

During the day, he would read and plan and talk to the tree. "I'll be famous, you know, when I see Santa's reindeer and sleigh. They'll bring cameras and TV crews. They'll talk about me all over the world. They'll probably even make a website. Everyone will want me as their friend. People will write blogs, send tweets…" He would go on and on.

When Ronald started back at school in the fall, Sherwin asked him if he wanted to work with him on a science project. No one had ever asked Ronald to work with them on anything. He asked Sherwin if he wanted to learn more about telescopes.

"Sure, that sounds cool."

So they got to work finding books and websites all about telescopes, how they worked, which was the biggest telescope in the world, and how to make one. One day, Ronald told Sherwin about Maple and his plan.

"If we make a good telescope and it works, do you think I could come and test it out with you on your platform in your tree?"

Ronald smiled wide. "Sure, that would be the best place to test it."

Then the winds began to change, birds gathered on the hydro lines, waiting to fly south together, and Ronald felt he was ready. As the cold winds of winter began to blow, up he went, getting his super-spy station ready for his Santa watch.

That year, as he waited on Christmas Eve, his longer legs dangling down between those now snug tip-top branches, his thermos of hot chocolate steaming between his mitted hands, he saw a brighter light in the sky. Quickly, he sat up, put down his cup, and peered keenly through his telescope at those millions of night stars, Christmas lights all over the sky. Something was different; something was happening. And then he saw it... eight bright lights in a row with a bigger light at the front. He couldn't believe it. He wished Sherwin were here to see this.

"Yes, yes... I knew it, I knew it was real. I found it, I found it," he cheered as he hugged his tree, his breath hanging in the frosty night air like a shiny Christmas tree ornament. He grabbed his special camera with night vision (another Christmas present from Grandma Cora last year) that attached to the end of his telescope and took as many pictures as he could.

That Christmas Eve, he didn't need extra hot chocolate to keep warm. He carefully put away his telescope, nimbly made his way down the tree, went into the house and climbed into bed to dream of the twinkling night sky.

The next morning, he came downstairs excited to tell his story, and there, under the family Christmas tree with a big red bow tied around it, was a framed picture of the eight bright night-lights he had seen just the night before... the picture HE had taken of Santa and his reindeer from the top branches in his tree. It was magic. The magic of believing. Christmas magic. Ronald sat down and hugged the picture to his chest. He had done it. He wondered what Mrs. Rothwell would say.

There is one chestnut tree on Primrose Street, amidst the forest of maples that majestically stand watch over homes. It stands outside Twenty Primrose Street, near Ruth's house. Jessica and Phil used to play under the tree as children. They loved to collect the blossoms in the spring, and Phil would make flower crowns for Jessica. The tree marvelled at the games the two played and would sprinkle them with more flowers for fun.

She would be the princess, and he chose to be the jester rather than the prince. The tree would adorn them with fragrant, white flowers. Often there were so many blooms that Jessica could lie on the ground and Phil would cover her with the wispy white petals until only her toes were exposed. Then it would be his turn, and she would bury him. They would sit and talk and play until lunch, when one of their mothers showed up with a picnic lunch for them: egg salad sandwiches, two cans of ice tea, a sliced apple to share, and two granola bars with the little marshmallow bits they both loved. They would spread out the fare on the white carpet of chestnut whites and take their time. On hot days in the summer, they set up a lemonade stand together, splitting the proceeds equally, twenty cents each.

After grade four, Jessica went to a different school, and they played together less and less often. Jessica would sometimes sit at her kitchen table and watch the chestnut limbs bending gracefully under seasonal winds, remembering how she played with Phil, regretting how growing up can change things. She would wave when Phil would ride by on his bike, and sometimes they would stop, sit together and lean against the bark of the chestnut, and chat for a bit. As they got older, more and more things took their time away from each other, and the chestnut tree.

The tree continues to throw blossoms on the ground each spring. It continues to bend with breezes. It continues to throw its shade over the lawn and the house and the street. Her large limbs reach out and around, like a big mama protecting her little ones. But even the fiercest of mothers cannot stop time, cannot turn it back, and cannot choose for her babies.

TWENTY PRIMROSE STREET: JESSICA

It was hard to tell when it happened. When Jessica started to come unglued.

A conversation with her used to be entrancing, beguiling. Her eyes drew you in with their laughter, their intent to engage, their intensity, their yearning, and curiosity. It was easy to see the myriad words and ideas playing around in her head, the battle ongoing to determine which phrase would eventually win. It was a tease, guile, and she wrapped herself around you, making it hard to step away. The conversation floated around like milkweed seeds looking for a place to land. The hope was one of her seeds would plant itself close to you.

"Come on, come on. You know what it is, look at this line right here… right here." Jess was pointing emphatically.

"Jess, you're not supposed to talk when you draw. It's only the team guessing who talks."

"Well, that just makes no sense. I mean, if you are on the right track, fine, but otherwise I'm going to help with my words."

"Then everyone will do that."

"Great, let's change the rules, I love that." Everyone laughed. Even at a party game it was impossible not to be engaged when she started. Her laugh, her twinkly eyes, and her argument were so unique and passionate, how could you say no?

"Fine, we'll change the rules. Pictionary revisited."

"Awesome. Now, doesn't everyone just feel so much better?" Everyone laughed. Jessica's energy was infectious, and her eyes dared you with their sparkles like sun on a clear, calm lake in early morning.

Now, her eyes were like the ones painted on papier mâché puppets, large pupils staring in one direction, the whites large and looming around the dark iris. They tricked you into thinking they were always looking at you in their abject stillness. The shiny skin tones on her face reflected the lights from lamps, and the bright red mouth was slightly upturned, hints of happiness that disappeared when the lamps switched off.

In the rain, the puppet began to droop, scars of paint from the eyes and mouth streaking down and lipping over the chin. The eyelashes would fall off one by one, the dark eye's pupil diluting onto the skin tones, blurring in moisture. The mâché started to cave in with the weight of water, and shreds began to peel off and fall to the ground, unravelling the structure. A hand placed firmly on the puppet would crush it to nothing now, a ball of mess and glue and muddied paint. Indistinguishable. Unidentifiable. Muted. Unglued.

It probably wasn't one moment. Not one precise moment. Not like standing in a rain storm and watching a lightning bolt hit a tree, fracturing it instantly into two pieces. It was more like a series of defined moments. An accumulation of instances. A collection of experiences.

It may have begun as a young girl when she picked up the .22 rifle and pointed it at her father. That had been a precise moment. Her brother was hiding beside the couch while her father screamed and yelled abuse at the family, his ruddy red cheeks laughing at their fear. His hand was curled around the cool brown curved glass, bits of liquid jumping out in sprays when he jerked or lurched forward. Her mother was crying as she cradled her bruised cheek with her left palm. The midsized dog Spike barked and barked and barked from the doorway into the other room, knowing there was danger but wise enough to stay a distance away. He was crouched low, hair bristling along his back, teeth bared, head jutted forward, paws firmly planted in front, ready to protect or attack. Amidst the spiralling emotions, Jessica saw herself calmly move to the corner of the room, in a dreamlike dance, where sounds just knocked gently against the windows of her consciousness. She turned the tiny brass key that sat in the lock to the large wooden case. It was as tall as her, with oak doors varnished heavily, glass panels set inside each door so that you could easily admire the weaponry held on racks inside. It was still inside the case — quiet, unperturbed. The lock clicked under the key, and she opened one of the doors, feeling a slight resistance in the hinges. She pulled it open and stood for a minute in quiet contemplation. Then she slowly reached forward and took one rifle out of its holding place. She slid her hand down its barrel, soft and strong and smooth. She had shot ten cans in a row off the last time her dad had taken her out to practice at his friend's farm.

"You need to know how to shoot a gun, Jessica," she remembered her dad telling her just last week. "You never know when a wounded animal needs to be put out of its misery or an intruder needs a bullet in the knee. You just never know when you may need its company," he said, smiling like a thief before picking your pocket. "A gun is your friend. Remember that." Jessica nodded, never wanting to disagree with her father, since his temper could be quick and hostile. No one else in her grade eight class could fire a gun. He repositioned the cans along the top rail of the fence and handed her more bullets. "Don't miss this time." Jessica started to ready the gun. "No, no," her father yelled, "it only takes a moment to ready the gun. Too slow, and you'll shoot yourself instead of the target. Careful. Do it right." Jessica was nervously perspiring as she aimed at the cans, knocking every one over. She was always nervous around her father. He turned after she finished shooting and walked toward the car without a word. Jessica stood shaking slightly, the gun heavy in her hands.

Now she opened the small drawer that rested under the gun rack and loaded one bullet into the rifle. She didn't ready the gun; she just loaded it. She put an extra bullet into her pocket. Everything was slow motion now as she turned around to face the room. Her mother was now crouching near the floor, the glass that had been in her father's hand smashed on the floor beside her. He was walking over to her brother now. The dog was growling and biting at his heels, and he kept kicking it away. She moved into the centre of the room, her mother behind her, her father between her and the door that led outside. She lifted the gun to her shoulder and cocked it. The sound bellowed into the room like a cannon going off. She hadn't even fired yet; just the sound of the bullet sliding into place was enough. Her father stood up and faced her, silent, a speck of drool slipping out of the corner of his mouth. He put his hand up and spoke more softly as he began to walk toward her. She was confident of her ability. She said nothing, just aimed at his feet and fired. Then quickly reloaded, smooth, quick, agile. She held the gun up again, aimed at his head this time. Quietly, like the weapons waiting in their case, she spoke.

"Get out," she whispered, "get out." She took one step toward him. There was not a sound in the room. The dog was lying down now, ready to pounce, waiting for her cue. Her mother had her hands over her mouth, and her brother had crawled behind the couch. When her father didn't move, she cocked the gun.

"Get out now," she repeated slowly. He turned and walked out. She went over and locked the door. She walked to the corner of the room. She carefully put the gun back into its place on the rack, closed the glass-panelled door and turned the key in its lock. Her mother began to sob quietly. Her brother ran upstairs to his room, the dog close on his heels.

Maybe Adam had something to do with her decline. He had been in her science classes first year at university. Tall, short ginger hair, rocket blue eyes, wide shoulders, swimmer's legs. She caught him glancing at her during a lecture. He'd chuckle when she'd challenge the professor; she made the class exciting, worth attending. She had fire. They soon became a couple, drinking at the pub after class, studying late in the library, watching movies in the back row of the cinema. Then one Sunday morning she rolled over to kiss him.

"Jess." She was snuggled in his arm, her head on his chest, her right arm across his body.

"Hmmhmmm."

"I want to make love with you this morning. I don't want to wait anymore. You're making me crazy."

She turned her face up to his, and he kissed her mouth.

"Do you have a condom?" He reached over to the night table and produced said item, smiling.

"I don't know, Adam." She had pulled back and was leaning on her hand, her left elbow propped onto the bed, her breasts exposed as the sheet slid off her shoulder.

"Baby, don't you want to?"

"You know I do, it's just, well, I don't know, it's kind of sudden."

"Sudden? Jess, it's been months now." He slid his hand across the sheet underneath them and started to play with her nipple.

"Adam."

"Yes, baby."

"Do you love me?"

"What do you think this boner is saying?"

"You know what I mean." He leaned in and kissed her mouth, the other hand sliding up her thigh and pushing her legs apart.

"I love you, Jess."

She remembered it was a Sunday because of the bells chiming in the distance. She always felt their haunting echo was more of a warning than a call to worship. The window was open slightly, letting a cool breeze blow over her bare legs that slid out from under the thin pale blue sheet on the twin bed they both occupied. It was late spring, end of term. Her body craved him as he touched her, kissed her, and rushed to climb inside. She didn't remember joy or passion, only sadness, a loss. It was over before it began. She felt his warm semen running out of her onto the bed, and when she rolled over, she saw it was mingled with her virgin blood. He gave her bum a gentle slap as he rolled out of bed and started to get dressed. She wanted to cry and kept her face buried in the pillow.

"See you at class later?"

"Sure," she said, muffled.

They both did a summer semester together... dancing, sleeping, loving, studying, planning. She started to relax a little. But the sex was always quick, hurried, like he had something better to do. She never said anything, didn't know how, didn't know it could be any different except in stories or movies, and how real were they?

"Adam, my lease is up this fall, and you're not staying in residence anymore. Why don't we rent a place together?"

"Definitely makes sense, babe, but I think it's just too much too fast, you know what I mean. But let's exchange keys and then it's pretty much like we're living together. Okay?"

"Okay." There wasn't any discussion. He moved into a studio apartment in the fall, and she moved into a room in a house with three other women. One night after class, he said he'd be working late, so she decided to go over and take dinner, have a surprise for him when he got home. Dinner on the table, her naked in his bed. She stood in the hallway fumbling with her key, balancing the food in the crook of her other arm, and jiggled the key into the slot, opening the door with her foot. It was the fragrance that first hit her before she turned her head to see the bed, rumpled with long, dark brown hair falling over the footboard and short ginger hair buried inside it, glistening skin moving in rhythms with the mattress. They didn't even know she was there until the crook of her arm released and the containers smashed onto the floor, a mess of shattered glass and casserole pooling around her feet. Both heads on the bed lifted at the same time, the rhythm dead. Three pairs of eyes locked onto threads circling the room, threads connecting and colliding and unravelling like an unfinished piece of embroidery. The sound of glass shattering echoed through the room. She stepped on shards of glass when she turned, dropping the key into the casserole, and walked out the door. She transferred to UBC the next semester.

There were other toxic moments throughout the years. But the betrayal by her husband was the maple key that spun everything out of focus. The moment when her breath was taken away. One moment they were laughing as he chased her down the beach on their second wedding anniversary while vacationing in the south, waves playing catch at their feet, seagulls cheering them on. The next she was opening the door to their hotel room, and there was her husband Antonio in their bed with another man. But not just any man — a man they had both come to call a friend, a man who had dinner at their house, a man with whom she had shared her candy floss when they had all gone to the fair together, a man she had known in high school from her home town, a boy who had made flower crowns for her hair, the best man at their wedding. She thought she had seen him on the beach a few days before but couldn't understand what Phil would be doing there, so she decided she must have been mistaken.

She had met Antonio on a flight to Vancouver. He had been behind her in the line of passengers as they made their way through the tunnel to the aircraft. She had dropped her ticket, and when she turned to bend down and pick it up, Antonio had already retrieved it and was handing it to her with a smile. It caught her by surprise, the simplicity of the smile, the sincerity of it, the beauty in his eyes. She thanked him and moved toward the plane. He was sitting across the aisle from her, and they talked all the way to Vancouver. He was returning from visiting his big Catholic family south of the border, she from an adventure away from her smaller family in Southern Ontario. They talked about food, hobbies, favourite vacation spots. The long flight seemed like a few minutes. Once back on campus, they had met for dinners, had gone skiing together, and she had slowly and decidedly fallen in love. He was so attentive, so interesting, so fun. He was everything she'd ever dreamed of. Her friends called him dreamy and were all a bit jealous. They decided to get married after graduation. They moved in together for their last year. And now he was holding another man, and she didn't know why.

There had been inklings, but she had dismissed them. She had explained them away. They crawled under her skin like earwigs in a cob of corn. He had been late for their wedding and had been very out of breath when he showed up, a bit pale. He had just said it was such a big step and there was so much going on. Or after making love, how he would never hold her and just bask in the afterglow. He would race to the bathroom and wash his hands over and over again. And he never wanted to look at her making love; he always wanted her from behind so he couldn't see her face. He said it added to the mystery. Now she wondered if it allowed him to picture other men instead of her. And he was always a little too excited when Phil came over for dinner or joined them on an outing. He had been studying at UBC as well, and Antonio always said he was just so excited at the friendship. "What are the chances that the two of you come from the same town? My friend and the woman I love. Too much," he would say. She hadn't paid attention. She didn't want to know.

And yet she did love him. She didn't want to let him go, but it was like she was standing on wet sand pulling away underneath her, pulling her into the ocean of her tears. She couldn't see him anymore. She couldn't understand who she was, who she had been to him. There was only a blank whiteness — nothing. She pounded his chest, her cries absorbed by the gulls and the waves. She kissed his lips, but he pushed her back and held her at arm's length, longingly looking to his lover.

"Antonio, please, please say something," she gasped, pulling at his cheeks, trying to force the words she wanted to hear out of his mouth. "Tell me this is a mistake. Tell me you are mine, you love me, and we can work through this. Tell me. TELL ME. TELL ME," she screamed over and over again.

She dove over Antonio and started to punch Phil, screaming at him. "You fucking creep, you pig. I thought you were my friend. How could you do this to me, HOW COULD YOU DO THIS TO ME." Phil sat rocking, holding his knees to his chest, his head down. Antonio pulled her away.

She clung to Antonio, held him, and rocked with him as the sand and sea crept between them and around them, volumes and volumes of tears engulfing them.

"Just pretend I died," he said, pulling her arms away from him, tears spilling from his eyes. He left her in a ball on the bed, like a snail curled into its shell at the hint of danger, and he walked out of the hotel room with Phil beside him.

Now she sat, looking blankly at the computer screen in front of her at work, smiling vacantly when someone approached her. She felt like a puppet, a papier mâché puppet, going through the motions decided by someone outside herself. No one seemed to notice that the papier mâché around her eyes was drooping. It took a moment to see that her eyes didn't blink or that she had been wearing the same clothes for days. No one noticed. She mechanically went from task to task and said goodbye at the end of the day. No one noticed. No one heard. Busy, busy.

When she burned down the workplace, it was at night so no one would be hurt. She had wanted to set them free from the days of disconnection and lies. She wanted release from the mundane, heartless days of endless nothingness. Money was everything. Money was nothing.

When she burned down the church, it was because the lie of compassion had become too much for her to accept. Empty words that filled her puppet's head and those of the other puppets sitting silently in pews. Paying no heed to pain or discomfort in others. Spreading a sugary icing on every conversation and action. But the icing would soon drip off onto the tablecloth, leaving a sticky mess, hard to clean up. Her papier mâché fingers dripped to the ground as she lit the match. Really, she was just burning the place where puppets gathered to feel okay about putting that sugar coating on life. She was setting them free.

She had loved by accident and had been part of a train wreck. She felt like a puppet dancing on strings.

She felt tired as she walked into the flames.

The maple tree outside Twenty Primrose Street stands adjacent to the chestnut. Ruth owns a collection of bird feeders. She adds a new one to the trees each year. The branches hang low enough for Ruth to reach easily and are close to her kitchen window for easy viewing but far enough that the birds feel safe on their perch.

The maple is one of the older trees on the street, and some of the top branches don't have summer leaves any more. The town says the tree is starting to hollow and will have to come down soon. Ruth doesn't want it crashing through her roof one evening, but she doesn't want it gone. She inquires if there is some way to trim off excess branches first in order to save the tree.

Ruth loves the tree. She remembers how Jessica helped her to fill the feeders as a little girl. She would stand so patiently, a few seeds in her hand, waiting for the chickadees to come and sit in her palm to eat. Ruth would watch as she filled the feeders, waiting for her sweet little smile to begin pulling at the corners of her mouth when one little brave bird finally took a seed out of her hand. Jessica would turn her head oh so slowly, not to scare him away, and look to her mother with absolute joy.

It was the same look the day she married Antonio. Ruth wore a long, elegant burgundy gown, and Frank was in a tux. Antonio's mother wore a light blue pantsuit and his dad a dark blue suit. They were very animated, his mother flitting about adjusting everyone's ties, straightening skirts. His dad joking and laughing, hugging his sons and shaking hands.

Frank and Ruth stood to one side, smiling plastically. But Jessica was happy, so happy. Antonio had his four brothers as his best men, and Jessica's brother. Phil was also in the party. Ruth remembered him playing with Jessica when they were kids. A nice boy. She thought it was so funny that they had all connected so far away from home. Jessica had her two friends from school in her party and Antonio's two sisters. It was an elaborate wedding by Ruth's standards. Jessica looked beautiful in her off-the-shoulder dress with the little pearl buttons and the long, long train behind her. A princess. She held lilies as her bouquet, one breaking off as she tossed it in the air after the vows and rings. The cake was huge. There were guffaws and scream of laughter when Antonio missed her mouth posing for a picture and some of the cake slipped down the front of Jessica's dress. "Hey man, you're not on your honeymoon yet, leave it be," shouted one of his friends to cheers and jests from the crowd. She remembers wondering why Phil was the only one not laughing. The new couple danced so close together, toasted, kissed. Ruth danced with her son-in-law and thought how very charming he was, how lucky her daughter was to have caught him. Frank danced with Jessica, and they had a moment together. Then they were off with cans clanging behind the limo taking them to the airport for their honeymoon. It had been a glorious day. Ruth remembered it well.

Frank died of heart issues a few years back. There was no love lost between him and Jessica. The moment at her wedding hadn't stuck. It had been his third heart attack. After the first one, Jessica she said she hoped he would have an epiphany, like other heart patients she had read about. People who had felt grateful for a second chance and turned their lives into something different. Ruth remembered the book she had bought for Frank that talked about the right diet for a healthy heart and some meditative visualizations to stay healthy and peaceful. She knew Jessica had given it to him with the highest of hopes for a new start to their relationship. A week later, when she came to visit, all the food in the house had changed and Ruth was cooking recipes out of the book. Ruth remembered Jessica was quite excited.

"Wow, I'm so glad you found the book helpful, Dad."

"Well, the food seems to be a good idea, and Ruth is doing a good job figuring out those recipes."

"That's great, Mom. Let me help. How did you like the second part of the book, Dad?"

"What second part?"

"You know, the meditations, ways to stay calm and peaceful. That stuff. They say that a peaceful mind goes a long way to a healthy heart." Her mother smiled a tight, strained smile when she saw Jessica's confusion.

"Oh God, Jess, give it a rest. I'm not reading that patchouli Birkenstock crap. I don't need to be *that* calm. I'm peaceful enough. But the food's a good idea."

"Okay. Didn't it say that alcohol was a bad idea?"

"Yeah, so?"

"Well, isn't that a beer you're drinking, Dad?"

"It's non-alcoholic."

"It's says Labatt's Blue on the can."

"Who asked you to dinner again?"

Jessica started to toss and toss the salad, looking at Ruth.

Jessica didn't go to his funeral. Ruth knew she was always smoothing things over, trying to make him seem more sympathetic and interested than he ever really was. It never made a difference. She knew it all had taken a toll on Jessica, although she'd never admit to that. It wasn't Ruth's fault, of course. She took comfort in the fact that her daughter had found happiness. Found someone to love her and care for her like she deserved. Someone that would engage her smile, laugh with her, shower her with moments of tenderness. Hold her in moments of stress and sadness. Understand her.

Ruth was glad her daughter had found what had eluded her in her own life.

TWENTY PRIMROSE STREET: RUTH

Ruth made an extra effort to keep the bird feeders full in the winter. She knew Jessica would be looking for the chickadees when she got home from the hospital. She had been out of the ICU for a few weeks now and into a regular room. But she was still blank and weak. Not her old Jessica.

Ruth watched the feeders swaying in the winter wind from her kitchen window, snow glued in patches to the glass, snow pushing its way through arching evergreens, snow swirling like tumbleweeds across her yard, snow gathering in thick slices on the roof of the squirrel-proof bird feeder. She marvelled at the small creatures. They brought her pleasure in the lonely winter months. Jessica's belongings were still stacked box upon box in the guest room upstairs from when they arrived from out west.

The tiny birds clung to the feeder's perch as the little house swayed under the force of winter weather. Wind separated their breast feathers, revealing pinkish-grey skin. Beaks picked out the best seeds as their tiny heads darted from side to side, spying other hungry birds. They could squeeze four sparrows and one small chickadee onto the perch, but it got very cramped. It became like a crowded mall at Christmas. They started pushing and pecking each other, glimpsing waiting shoppers in the branches nearby, all vying for that last grain. Ruth knew there would be no Christmas shopping for her that year. She and Jessica had always made a day of it together, shopping, having lunch, maybe a few drinks. She remembered the call from down south. The call where Jessica was quietly hysterical.

"Mom, is that..." Sobs and blowing of a nose interrupted the words. "Is that you?"

"Jess? What is it? What's wrong?"

"He's gone... he's with Phil... the bed... his hair...." More sobs, more Kleenexes. "The spa and then, Mom, oh Mom..."

"Jess, I can't understand what you're saying. Are you hurt?" Ruth was getting a tight feeling all over her body. Something was very wrong.

"Yes, yes, I'm hurt... OH GOD, I'M HURT," she started wailing into the phone.

Bits and pieces of her words floated through the phone until Ruth understood what had happened. It would be a scandal. It was all she could think about. She was filled with adrenaline. She told Jessica to come home.

Antonio a homosexual. She felt sick. Disgusted. Her poor, poor Jessica. Such utter humiliation. What would she tell people? She went and got every photo album and cut out his head from every single snapshot. She put the mangled pictures back into their album slots and waited for Jessica to get home. She left the albums on the table, confident that it would pull Jessica in the right direction, free from the past. But Jessica had already stepped too far over the edge by the time she stepped off the plane.

When Ruth picked her up at the airport gate, it was a shock. Her happy Jessica was dragging her purse and luggage on the floor behind her. She was pale and walked as if on high doses of Valium. When she saw her mother, tears fell over her cheeks, but she made no move to hug.

After days of sleeping and eating very little of anything, Ruth was glad when Jessica said she wanted to get a job, that she was ready to leave the house. She took a job in a small coffee shop that sold knick-knacks and light lunches on Main Street in Martineville. It was a popular spot. Ruth felt it was time to show her what she had done to help. She proudly displayed the mutilated photo albums on the dining room table. She knew it would give knew it would give Jessica strength to see Antonio literally cut out of their lives. Jessica's face remained like the painted face of a puppet.

Ruth kept saying it would all be okay. She always said that.

They started going to church on Sunday. Ruth said it would be nice to dress up and thought it would soothe Jessica's soul. She spoke very little when she came home from work. When the police called Ruth, she wasn't really surprised. She was surprised by the extent of Jessica's burns. She would be in the hospital's ICU for months, she was told.

Ruth had trouble getting out of bed in the morning these days. She would just lie there listening to the weather outside and imagined the birds at their feeders. She went to the hospital and watched Jessica through the ICU window. Amanda, the doctor treating Jessica, saw her there one afternoon and came to sit beside her.

"Hi Ruth. How are you?"

Ruth turned, almost robotically. "I'm numb, Amanda. I'm numb."

"She'll be okay, Ruth; she isn't going to die. The burns are healing really well. You'll be able to sit with her very soon, and then she'll be home."

"On house arrest, I'm told."

"Well, that won't be forever. It will give you both time to catch up and heal."

"Yes, I guess. Just thank God that no one else was hurt. Just all seems like a bad dream I can't wake up from."

"I've had those kinds of days too, Ruth. Believe me. I still have nightmares when I think of Derek's room. It will be okay." Amanda heard her name called over the PA system.

Dr. Taylor, report to ICU 5 please, report to ICU 5.

"Sorry, Ruth, that's me. I have to go. You can see Jessica tomorrow. Meantime, really try to get some rest. She's going to need you when she comes home."

"Thanks, Amanda." She pulled herself out of the chair and made her way out of the hospital and down the road toward Primrose Street. Once home, she would draw herself a bath. Ruth enjoyed the bath. She would lie in the warm, comforting water, feeling her numb body come to life, listening to the soft song of the bubbles around her. She thought of the little finches, so bright and separate from the other birds. The finches seemed removed from it all. They had their own small red feeder filled with thin black seeds. They were the only ones who savoured this avian comestible. They observed the other frantic shoppers whilst sitting in their café, leisurely sipping Nyjer birdseed lattes as snowflakes whisked by.

They seemed much more civilized in how they shared their feeder with those waiting on wings. The sparrows were very pushy, not willing to share or wait in any line. And the blue jays were so big, they just took what they wanted when they wanted it. But the little chickadees, they were Ruth's favourite, same as Jessica. They would sit in the branches of nearby trees, singing chic-a-dee-dee-dee and waiting until the feeding frenzy was over, then politely take their turn on the feeder, pecking away.

She liked the gentle poofing sound the bubbles made as they started to dissipate in the bath water. She moved her hand back and forth, enjoying the movement it made over her skin.

Ruth pulled herself out of the bath, dried herself off, and slipped into her robe and slippers as she made her way downstairs. She turned on the TV, just in time to watch Oprah. She remembered moving into the house years ago, and Oprah was the first thing she watched then. She had thought things would be so different when they moved into this house. Her husband didn't have far to drive to work anymore, and she had found a good job as a legal secretary. Yet Frank only seemed happy behind the controls, up in the basket fixing electrical wires. His temper flared so easily and so quickly. His drinking never helped. Ruth had often thought of leaving him, but she made very little at her job. She was afraid she wouldn't be able to make ends meet and that the kids would suffer. Frank's job allowed them to have material things, vacations, and nice vehicles. So she stayed, resigned to weather the storms and find solace on sandy warm beaches in winter and European architecture in summers. When Frank died, he left her a lot of debt, a cancelled life insurance policy but a solid pension.

Ruth got up to make some tea. Dr. Phil was on after Oprah. She would have to remember to fill the bird feeders later.

The large tree in the backyard carefully screens the view from their house to Charlie's shop. But Charlie likes it that way. He likes the privacy the tree affords him. Cora has to dart her eyes between branches and leaves to try to see him back there, until she finally gives up and just uses the intercom he installed. The Burkes have lived at Twelve Primrose Street for almost sixty years. They married as high school sweethearts. They have one of the biggest lots on the street, big enough for Charlie to have built a very large workshop for his many ongoing, never-finished, keep-busy projects. Charlie worked for the city for years, and when he retired he started to build his workshop. It keeps him alive. His son, Tom, comes and works with him. It's their together time. He lives just down the road. Charlie often goes and helps Tom with building projects, fix-up projects, and Tom returns the favours. Ronald, his grandson, is getting better and better at helping with things. Charlie pitched in a few times when Tom and Ronald were building an elaborate treehouse in the backyard. And Ronald visits and bakes cookies with Cora and just talks up a storm. He is a sweet boy, quiet, polite, and always willing to help. Their two daughters live down in the States now, so they don't get to see their other children or grandchildren very often. But they feel like Primrose Street is their real family.

Charlie and Cora were like adopted grandparents to Derek and his sister Amanda from down the street, and they loved that. They came to their house every day after school when they were small. Cora made sure she had lots of crayons and colouring books around. Derek loved to colour. He wasn't too concerned with staying inside the lines and using orthodox colours for different scenes. He'd colour dogs blue, trees pink and purple, houses red with blue dots, people a very light blue, and skies multicoloured, like rainbows scattered all over. Cora saved all his colouring books. Amanda was more precise about her colouring. She stayed carefully inside the lines and used accepted colours for skies and animals. Cora took photographs of the kids, lots of them. Amanda and Derek were so cute. She has pictures of them eating snacks at the kitchen table, colouring together, their lemonade stand one summer, and the food fight that Charlie started when they were picnicking in the backyard. There was icing everywhere, on everyone. Cora also has a toy collection she started for her grandchildren: a pirate ship, a dollhouse, and a tractor set, and Amanda and Derek loved them. Derek always chose the dollhouse. He could sit for hours and talk to himself, rearranging furniture in the house, dressing and redressing the dolls. His sister liked the tractor set. She helped Derek arrange the garden in front of the dollhouse using the little tractors.

But Derek was quiet. Very quiet. Cora would ask what he'd want for a snack, and he'd look up at her with his huge brown eyes, like a fawn in the headlights, and say nothing. A few times, Charlie and his booming voice made Derek cry. Charlie would feel just awful, and he'd go and sit on the floor with Derek and tell him softly that everything was okay. Cora always worried about Derek.

When the kids got older, they would still visit Charlie and Cora after school, and Cora would drag out the colouring books, the cookies, and milk. Even Charlie would sit and colour with them. It never got old. And then it was just Charlie and Cora.

Charlie and Cora created a good life together, a house that is warm and inviting, and a marriage that still has sparkle after almost sixty years. Everyone on the street looks at them with wonder.

TWELVE PRIMROSE STREET: CHARLIE AND CORA

Charlie Burke still went to work out in his shop every day. He had built the shop out back years ago for when he retired so he'd have a place to fix up his vehicles, work on broken pieces of furniture and interesting things he'd find at the dump just outside of town … and to have his own space. The walls of his shop were lined with shelves holding a variety of jars with different sized nails and screws. Large tools hung from hooks: saws, axes, chainsaws. There was a fridge in one corner and a cupboard he had rescued from the dump out of town, filled with snacks. There was a wood stove in the corner of the shop and enough room in the centre for a vehicle or small tractor. There was wood stacked along the wall outside to keep him warm all winter while he worked. He had a wood splitter behind his shop that kept him busy all fall, getting large summer logs ready for his wood stoves during winter winds. An old stereo, his best dump find to date, stood on the shelf on the far left wall, where Barry Manilow or Celine Dion would wail a tune in rhythm to his work, keeping him company. The same CD over and over and over again.

Cora was happy to get Charlie out of the house each day. They had bought their property years ago when Martineville was still small and lots were still huge. She had resented having so much grass to cut during the years of children, diapers, and jobs. But now it was enough space for a shop, which ate up most of the grass and gave Charlie something to do. She was grateful for the huge lot. With Charlie in the shop she had her time to talk with friends and family and keep up with the local gossip. That's when she'd crank up the country music tunes and sing along while she created her culinary delicacies for the day. She loved to cook. Although Cora was finding it a little hard to hear these days, her eyes were still keen. Their aquamarine blue saw through any nonsense. And she was as sharp as the knife she used to slice her tomatoes.

Red rounds of happiness dotted each cheek, and her now thinning blonde/grey hair was cut short for easy care. It was a compact kitchen where counter space was at a premium, but she knew where everything was and wouldn't change a thing. Charlie had offered to give her a bigger kitchen with new appliances. But she had baked the wedding cake for their daughter's wedding in that kitchen and countless birthday cakes over the years, not to mention Christmas and Thanksgiving dinners. She would admit it was tiny and cramped, but there were just too many memories. Cora continued to cook for everyone in her tiny but perfect kitchen. She made pies and tarts, brownies and soups, chili sauce and jams, and there always seemed to be someone around happy to pick up a fork or a spoon or take a jar or platter of goodies.

Charlie had installed an intercom system from the house to the shop the day he retired so Cora could call him for meals throughout the day without having to go outside. She'd been preparing meals for Charlie since she was nineteen and didn't know what she'd do without the old windbag. Charlie loved to tell stories. Cora had heard every story more than a hundred times but would sit patiently when they had visitors, smiling at her Charlie, correcting him at the same point in each story, while he wove his way through the tale again and again.

Cora set the table, had the tea steeping and the soup cooling on the table, the bread sliced, and the pickles plated before she hollered up to Charlie on the intercom.

"Supper's ready."

"What time is it?"

"It's 12:45."

"Well, supper isn't until one. I have fifteen minutes left."

"Well, if you start walking now, you'll be here by one then." Intercom out. He happily grumbled all the way to the house. Even though the distance was short, everything seemed to take a long time these days.

"Smells good, Cora girl." She gave his shoulder a squeeze of thanks as he lowered himself into his chair, his knees aching.

"Doctor called, you have your check-up today at two."

"Hate those damn doctors. They always make me feel old."

"You *are* old." They laughed together.

"Not too old to still keep you happy, girl. Heeeehaw," he wailed and leaned over to kiss her on the cheek and steal a quick squeeze. She responded with the appropriate look of disdain but loved every minute of it. Truth was, making each other happy "like that" wasn't quite as easy as it used to be. They didn't talk about it; they had other things to share now.

"We'll leave after lunch then," she said.

"No time to 'play'?" he asked, lifting up one eyebrow.

"No, Charlie, it just takes too long to get to the car, and we have to be on time. Anyway, you know all the parts aren't too happy to play anymore."

"Oh, fine." And he grumbled his way through his supper.

The doctor was a fifteen-minute drive from their home. There was a new young doctor, Murphy, at the clinic. She had seen Charlie and Cora a few times. For their age, they were both in good health, but their joints were starting to wear out. And Cora was worried about Charlie's blood pressure. Charlie and Cora didn't like getting old.

"Well, Mr. Burke, other than things taking a bit longer to get moving, you are doing very well. I don't need to see you for another six months... unless you call. Did you have any questions for me?"

"Well, now that you mention it, you know, things taking a bit longer to get moving and all, I was wondering about trying some of that VeeAgaara I saw on TeeVee?"

"Viagra... really. Well, sure. I'd be careful though. Can be hard on your heart. I'll give you two pills and cut them into four pieces each. That should last a while. You'll probably only need one quarter each time, you know, to get things moving." She smiled.

She handed him the pills.

"I'm giving you a couple so you can see how they work, Charlie, and if you like it, you know. But if you decide to buy more, they're not covered on your plan, and they are pretty pricey."

"You're kidding me. Like how pricey?" Charlie guffawed.

"Well, it depends on dose, etc., but between twenty and fifty dollars for one pill."

"ONE PILL. Jesus, that's what I'd pay for groceries for a month."

"Well, make these last then. And if it's working, I'll see what I can do." She winked and gave Charlie a nudge.

"I better not get too happy about this, eh?"

The doctor smiled. "Well, you have enough there for at least eight exciting moments. But do remember, I've cut them into four pieces and just take one piece for each time. Give it a few minutes too; it won't happen immediately, so do some preparation. Know what I mean?"

"I'm imagining," he said with a cheeky grin.

"Okay, well, let me know how it goes." She smiled as he left her office.

Cora was waiting in the car at the front of the clinic when Charlie came out. He slid into the passenger seat, leaned over and kissed her on the cheek, then whispered, "I have a surprise for you, Mother," and then settled smugly back into his seat as Cora drove on, looking confused and curious, her lips pursed and a little turned up on one side.

Charlie took one quarter of a pill the next morning up in his shop. He was hoping for some fun after lunch that day. He went about fixing a chair, his task for that day, very aware of his pants just below his belt buckle and hoping for some activity. After half an hour and nothing new happening, he took another quarter pill. He began sanding a spindle of wood for a chair he was fixing, worked at it for quite a while — nothing — so he took the other half of the pill.

The intercom buzzed and crackled. "Lunch, Charlie."

"Damn," cursed Charlie to himself, "these bloody pills don't do a thing." And he stuffed another quarter pill into his mouth as his old joints creaked their way down to the house.

Cora had her feast fanned out on the table, salad and six different choices of salad dressing, beef barley soup, bread, and the teapot.

The peach cobbler for dessert was cooling on the counter. Charlie sat down and waited for Cora.

"Stella was moved to that horrible old folks' home this morning," Cora began. "She says it's like jail. Poor thing," she muttered as she poured tea into their mugs. "I said we'd come and visit her tomorrow. I'm going to bake a pie to take to her. I'll make a peach pie, she loves that, doesn't she, Charlie?"

"Yes, she does, it's her favourite all right, was her Fred's favourite too, God rest his soul." They sat quietly for a moment. So many of their friends were dying or being moved into homes where they didn't want to go. As Charlie buttered his bread, he thought about how much he enjoyed having supper with his Cora each day and was grateful he could still go to work out in his shop. He was getting more and more excited about his surprise. Cora got up to put more hot water in the teapot. It was not as easy for her to move around, but she was so grateful to be in her own kitchen, still setting the table for two. It was such a strange point in life, so close to death but so alive.

"I'll just go into downtown after lunch and get some peaches. You need anything?"

"No honey, I'm good. You be careful, though, they sure drive fast these days."

"Oh, Charlie, you know I drive like an old lady."

"That's true. I'll be lucky if I see you for dinner."

And their conversation went on and on. It was always like that with them, interested in what the other said. They wanted to listen to each other.

Cora started cleaning up the dishes, and Charlie started putting on his boots. The clear division of labour was comfortable for them both.

"What was that surprise, Charlie? You still haven't told me."

"I'll tell you later, Mother." And he was out the door and off to work at the shop. He was disappointed. He would have to wait until after dinner now, but then it was hard to stay awake. Maybe after his nap, after Cora finished making her peach pie.

In his shop, he had the chair firmly fixed into the clamps and had ·just found the glue to attach the new spindle when he felt the quiver in his loins. He stood up straight, as straight as his back allowed, glue bottle in one hand, spindle in the other. He stood absolutely still, as if waiting to hear that one tree fall deep in the bush. The quiver was now a tingle. He looked down at his pants just below his belt buckle. They were moving ever so slightly, and then, not so slightly.

"Sweet Mother of Jesus."

He dropped the glue bottle. He dropped the spindle and headed for the door, not sure how long the "surprise" would last. He opened the shop door and started calling, "Cora, Cora girl, I've got that surprise now, I've got your surprise!"

And as he rushed along the path to the house, his joints creaking and complaining, breathless with anticipation and lack of oxygen, and yearning for his sweetheart, he saw their red Honda Civic pulling out of the garage with Cora behind the wheel.

He froze. "Peaches, goddamn peaches." He couldn't run. Cora couldn't hear him. The Civic poked along Primrose Street and out of sight. And Charlie stood between the house and the road, panting, his wasted surprise pulsing in his pants.

As the wind blows and bends the tree at Twenty-Two Primrose Street, shooting pains splinter up and down the trunk. The pain happens consistently since it was hit by lightning a few summers back. The crack echoed down the street, bringing people running onto the sidewalks. As the tree was ripped open, scorched black by the energy burst, the residents caught their breath. It had been split right down the centre, and yet it continues to live. When Rebecca now stands at her kitchen window, her thoughts are framed by the fissure in the tree as she looks into her past.

Rebecca recognizes that since the kids have both left home, she has grown apart from Peter. Even though she loves him, there is always a feeling that something is left unsaid between them, unspoken. She never mentions anything, because she isn't sure if it is her own guilt at how it all began. A secret she has kept locked up tight for years. Gaining a man at the expense of a friend maybe comes at a high price. It always sits in the back of her mind. She broke the code, the code between sisters.

She and Stephanie had been close. They had just finished university and were working at their first jobs. After work, they would meet at one apartment or the other, open a bottle of wine, and sit in the kitchen sipping and snacking and sharing. Usually the conversation would turn to men they'd met at work, on the bus, at the coffee shop. How the men may have looked in a pair of jeans, how they imagined they looked with no jeans at all. Size of chest, shape of ass, whether they imagined they could kiss like a saint or just inhale a woman's face. Sometimes they would take their wine to the bedroom and flop down beside each other on the bed, tell stories, laugh, giggle. They'd share clothes and try things on for each other.

"You really should have this dress of mine, Bec. I don't have enough to fill the front out like you do."

"True, your boobs are pretty small."

Stephanie opened her eyes wide. "Hey, I can say that but…"

"Wait, I wasn't finished… you have great nipples." And she reached up and pinched one of them.

"Hey, that hurt." They wrestled on the bed. Stephanie rolled over and propped herself up on one elbow. "So, want the dress?"

"Absolutely."

Silently, with slow movements as if in an underwater dream, their lips found each other's and they kissed for minutes, hands resting on the bed. They never wanted more than that kiss; they both loved men. But they loved each other too, and spending time together was important to them both.

"Want to wear that sexy dress tonight?" Stephanie rolled off the bed.

"Sure, what are you going to wear? Wait, let me pick." Rebecca went over to the closet and picked out a very sheer light blue blouse and tight-fitting jeans with white high heels.

"This will turn some heads, but don't wear a bra." They smiled at each other and got ready to go out.

Stephanie saw him first in the bar that evening while Rebecca had excused herself to find the ladies' room. When she returned, Stephanie was intently engaged with a man sitting beside Becca's stool. He had sandy brown hair that fell to his shoulders, a broad chest, muscular arms, and green eyes that rivalled a forest reflected in a Northern Ontario lake. Rebecca was riveted. She stood beside Stephanie for a moment before placing a hand on her shoulder.

"Oh, Bec, you're back. Sorry, we've taken your seat."

"No worries," said Becca, but the man was already pulling up another stool for her.

"Hi, I'm Peter."

He extended his hand, and when she connected with his skin, she felt a surge of energy course through her body. She shivered in response. "Hi," was all she could manage.

Stephanie was animated for the rest of the evening, and Peter's stool was pulled closer and closer to her own, leaving Becca to share her drink with the hockey game on the screen above the bar. Occasionally they would look in her direction, drawing her into the conversation, and she would laugh on cue, but she was caught between her desire for Peter and loyalty to her friend. She watched the ritual as Stephanie tossed her hair, imperceptibly stroked her fingers against Peter's arm, licked her lips with longing, uncrossed and recrossed her legs in slow motion like a cat stalking its prey.

When they left after last call, Stephanie was giggling all the way home. They were both tipsy, to say the least. She had begun her journey into Peter, and as days passed, Becca was forced to listen to intimate details of their dates as their relationship developed. Often, they would go out together, Peter bringing different friends for Becca. But since Becca was smitten with Peter, no date was quite good enough.

They all met for dinner one evening, and Peter began telling Stephanie about this craft festival in Toronto that he wanted to take her to.

"Hey, why don't we all go?" said Stephanie.

"Sure, great idea. You in, Bec?"

"You sure I'm not interfering?"

"Not at all, it'll be fun. Whatta you say."

"Sure, I'm in. This weekend?"

"Yeah, we'll leave early and stop for breakfast on the way. Sound good?" and the evening continued.

When Saturday rolled around, Becca was getting ready when the phone rang.

"Bec, I can't go."

"Why, what's up?"

"I just feel terrible. I have to keep running to the bathroom and feel horrible."

"Do you want me to come over? Shall I call and tell Peter we have to cancel?"

"No, he already bought the tickets. Listen, do you mind if I don't go? Can you still go so it isn't a total loss?"

"You sure, Steph?"

"Yeah, oh shit, I have to go again. Have fun, call me when you're back. Agghh."

Becca sat holding the phone in her hand. She felt numb and wrong about what she was going to do, but desire outweighed any other motivating factor. She dialled Peter's number and told him the situation. He eventually agreed, after giving Stephanie a call himself, and said he'd be by to pick her up in about twenty minutes. After he hung up, Becca went to get dressed and heard the machine pick up when the phone rang. She heard Stephanie's voice.

"Hey, girl, I think I'm feeling a bit better. If you haven't already left, give me a call and I'll tag along." It was the days before everyone had a cellphone.

Becca stood looking at the machine for a long time and walked out the door to meet Peter.

They started out the day as friends, with Stephanie buffered between them, but by the late afternoon they had been forced to stand very close together in a lineup. Becca was keenly aware of Peter's body close to hers. She could smell his aftershave, and it made her a bit light-headed. He turned to ask her a question, his face centimetres from her own, and when she moved in a little closer as he spoke, he leaned in to her lips. It was a glance at first, and then he looked at her, and the next time their lips met it was intentional and passionate. Peter's arm moved around her waist and pulled her close. She moaned ever so slightly at the feel of his body next to hers. When they stood apart, still in the line, they stayed standing very close to each other. Through the rest of the day, they moved within inches of each other. Peter fed her bits of food across the table. She reached for his fingers; he stroked her face. She never wanted the day to end.

On the way back in the car, Becca broke the dream. "What will we tell Stephanie?"

"That a threesome would be great? Sorry. Yeah, Steph. I don't really know." And he slid his hand under her dress as he continued to drive, stroking her legs, making her very wet with desire. She moaned, resting her head back, enjoying where he kept his hand. Her desire, her craving shadowed her reason and accountability. "Steph's great. Really great. I don't know. Let's talk about it later."

Peter didn't drive her home; he drove right to his place, parked, and escorted Becca into his house and down the hall to his bedroom. There was little to be said as clothes dropped to the floor and Peter expertly unclipped her bra, as they fell together onto the bed. They were wrapped around each other in minutes, skin and breath and moisture and moans and clawing and grasping until it all intermingled to a moment of exhale and they lay back, panting, waiting.

"Wine?" asked Peter as he pulled on his pants and shirt and went into the kitchen.

"Sure," Becca answered, putting on her clothes, feeling a bit shaky and luxurious all at the same time.

They sat at the kitchen table, sipping wine, nibbling bits of cheese Peter had produced, when they heard a car pull up, and the front door opened.

"Hello," called a voice. They both looked at each other as Stephanie walked around the corner. The gleam of sex burned around their edges, like a piece of wood charred and smouldering after a brief but intense fire. Breath and words dangled from webs entwining the three as they hovered in the room. Nobody dared to pull down the web and move forward.

"I thought you might be back earlier," ventured Steph. "I stopped by earlier, but you were still out." She moved around the table and leaned down to kiss Peter. He pulled out a chair for her and offered her a glass of wine.

"So how was the day? Was the event worthwhile?"

"More importantly, are you feeling better?" he asked as he brought her a glass and lightly touched her shoulder. Becca was quietly absorbed in her glass of wine, wishing there was more in it so she could slowly drown herself.

"Still a little queasy, but fever and headache is gone."

"Oh, that's good," said Becca. "You really didn't sound very good, and it was a lot of walking today."

"We can always go again if you like," said Peter. "Or try something else. You let me know what you'd like to do."

"Okay, well, thanks for the day, Peter, and the wine, I should be going."

"Do you want a ride?" offered Peter.

"No, I'll just take a cab." She walked around the table and gave Stephanie a hug. "Call me tomorrow, okay?"

"Sure thing." They both smiled, tight lines across their faces like boat lines drawn taut in a mooring as winds increased with the approaching storm.

"Thanks again, Peter." She waved as she left the kitchen and closed the outside door behind her. She stood for a moment, leaning back against the door, finally taking a full breath. She began to devise her plan to get Peter.

TWENTY-TWO PRIMROSE STREET: PETER

Peter and Rebecca Taylor had lived at Twenty-Two Primrose Street for over twenty years. Rebecca did landscape design in the summer and worked with the horticultural society in the winter. The garden in her front yard on Primrose Street was spectacular. Flagstone paths led the viewer from one flower to another, one herb to the next. A small bridge hovered over a river of tiny white and blue stones. Little gargoyles were positioned in key places, and bird feeders hung on cast iron rods pushed into the ground. Small benches invited one to sit and absorb, reflect. She had been working on the garden for years. It was her sanity, especially since the children had grown and moved into their own lives. When she wasn't actually in the garden, she was planning her next moves at the kitchen table. Rebecca was a slight woman, slim and attractive. She often had her long light brown hair pulled back into a ponytail that accentuated her soft, hazel eyes and striking bone structure. It was the feature that Peter had first noticed and was drawn to when he first saw her all those years ago.

Peter had recently become a member of the municipal council. He planned on running for mayor in a year. He had learned a lot about his community as a real estate agent, a cub-scout leader, a hockey parent, and a driver for Sylvia's gymnastic competitions. The community had come to trust him. It was the logical next step for him to become mayor.

In his personal life, things had become strained and difficult with Rebecca. It became magnified when both the kids finally left for university. But it had started long before that. Maybe there had always been a disconnect between them, and the children had provided enough distraction and effort that it wasn't noticed. Of course, there had been attraction. Peter remembered it well and how she had captivated him. It had been wild and great for a long time. But when he thought about it now, their sex life had become awkward, half measured. And it didn't happen often enough for him. Peter knew his wife liked to be touched; she just didn't seem to like it too often anymore. And she didn't like oral sex, in either direction. Rules were clear. There was more to marriage than sex, he'd tell himself. They did everything else so well together: parenting, throwing great parties, holidays, travelling, managing the house. But they didn't talk, not really, not about things that mattered. Everyone saw them as the perfect couple, the million-dollar family to be coveted.

Peter loved his family. He loved his wife. He knew she would watch him as he cleaned their pool in the backyard. He could see her peeking through her kitchen drapes while cooking dinner.

At night, as they positioned themselves into the bed they shared, there were times when Rebecca would run her hand across Peter's chest and then slide her hand down to his groin, her fingers playing with his pubic hair as his erection grew. He would reach for her breast and soon move over her. She would moan and grab his skin, hold him tightly as he entered her and cling to him as she came. Then wait as he pushed into his climax. When they rolled over, it was as if a switch was flipped. The moment of connection and vulnerability was quickly erased. Rebecca would begin to talk of items to be achieved the next day: who was driving where, what needed to be picked up. Peter would lie there, feeling dropped, alone. He never said anything. It would just turn into an argument. She just didn't want to hear him, it seemed. He knew they wouldn't make love again for weeks, and when they did it would be exactly the same. It always played out the same way. Rebecca would roll over, go through her list for the next day, and fall asleep. Peter would lie staring at the ceiling for most of the night.

He could see it was harder for Rebecca with the kids gone. Empty nest syndrome had had her in its claws for a long time, and there was little he could do. He had become invisible. He thought that since she wasn't talking with the kids as much, he and she would start talking together more, move closer. He saw how she occupied herself with the gardens and began volunteering more with the horticultural society in town. His illusion of connection was becoming a delusion. He realized that. Peter began working later into the evenings, coming home when she was already asleep. The sumptuous leftovers that used to greet him in the fridge after a long day were nowhere to be found. He was lucky to find cream for coffee.

Peter began to drink. Just a few at lunch, a couple in the deafening quiet of the house late at night. It allowed him to move through his days in a gentle fog, and things took a softer edge, like cookies dipped in milk. He began to stay at the office longer. Terrell usually worked late too, so he had company. Council meetings took a lot of preparation, and there was no point in going home. There was little there for him these days, or at least he had lost the energy to look. Terrell and Peter would share a few drinks while putting together a policy, share laughs and stories. It made Peter feel needed. And Terrell was very focused. He was always adamant about points he felt were needed and rarely backed down. Peter felt himself deferring to him more and more. He began to enjoy the feeling of not being in charge, not having to be the one to make decisions all the time.

After putting the finishing touches on a new proposal one evening, Terrell suggested ordering pizza and picking up a case of beer. Conversation flowed, and so did the beer. So, when Terrell reached over to grab another slice of pizza and his hand grazed Peter's, there was a natural progression. They both hesitated, allowing the moment to hover as their eyes searched the room, finally resting on each other. Terrell let his hand move down to Peter's belt buckle, and Peter didn't stop him. He needed to be touched, wanted. And he wanted to know what it was like to have someone else make the move. Terrell took Peter's hand and moved it to the zipper on his trousers. He firmly took Peter's arm, guiding him to his knees on the floor. Peter was intoxicated with the feeling, the alcohol swimming through his skin, his lips numb. He was swimming in a fishbowl.

The next morning, he was quiet drinking his coffee as Rebecca silently moved across the kitchen floor.

"Are you planting with the society today?" he asked her. Rebecca turned her head slowly, tipping it to one side, like someone trying to understand an unfamiliar sound.

"Yes." She couldn't find any other words.

"Would you like to grab some lunch today?"

"I'm going out to plan a garden today." She had nothing else to offer. Peter didn't try to find more of his words either.

He stayed late again that night with Terrell. They explored more of each other. It was exciting, something he longed for, and it was different. He'd had opportunities to sleep with Beth, one of the council women. She had made it clear she was very open to the idea. Beth was very sexy: long legs, long, dark blonde hair, exposed, voluptuous breasts, short skirts, high heels. Peter had often masturbated while thinking of her in various places, with varying degrees of clothing. But he had never considered another man. That had all just happened. That's what the allure was, the turn-on.

When they had pleasured each other to satisfaction, they leaned back and opened a beer.

"Peter," said Terrell, "what about Rebecca?" Peter sipped his beer methodically. "What is this about?" Terrell asked, motioning between them with his hand.

"Being wanted, touched, stimulated, I guess."

"Rebecca, she doesn't give you that?"

"Not often. She doesn't really notice me now that the kids are gone. Maybe she never really did. I always thought I was a bit of a trophy win for her. I don't know. What about your wife?"

"It's complicated." He paused, sipping his beer. "Peter, I'm gay."

"Does your wife know?"

"I don't think so."

"That is complicated. I'm not gay."

"I know."

"I love my family."

"I know that too. So, do I." He put down his beer can. "Is this over, Peter?" He choked on his words.

"I think so."

They continued drinking their beer and talking deep into the night. They kissed when they said goodnight, like lovers knowing it is the end. Knowing they will still work together.

As Peter drove home, he felt like Terrell had looked through his windowpane, into his deepest thoughts. It had been good to talk, really talk. But he knew things had changed for him; the glass had been irrevocably scratched.

He quietly entered his house, trying to collect himself. He stood looking at himself in the bathroom mirror. He saw a broken man struggling to find the missing piece. He wanted to make love to his wife. The shower could wait.

He crawled into bed beside Rebecca, sound asleep and snoring. He watched her. He wanted her. Her softness, her movement, her body under his. He so hoped they could find more together. Maybe start again.

He began to lightly caress her skin until she moved ever so slightly. He began to kiss her shoulder, trace his tongue up her neck to her ear, and she moaned slightly, turning toward him. Not a word needed to be spoken. He put his mouth on hers and began to kiss tenderly, slowly opening her mouth with his tongue and waiting for hers. She put her arms around his neck and kissed him back, pulling him closer. Her body rose to him. No words, just yearning and movement. He got on top, hard with desire, and slid inside her as she arched her back and moved under him for more. She cried out and clung to him, pulling him closer. They found a rhythm, like a sea approaching a storm. Afterward, they lay, breathless, covers at their feet and on the floor. He so hoped she wouldn't start talking about plans for the next day. Just once he wanted the moment to linger. He wanted to tell her that next time, he wanted to just roll her onto her side, spoon her, take her in the kitchen, over the end of the couch. He wanted to be erotic with her. He wanted to talk to her about all his thoughts. He wanted them to find their marriage.

He reached over, inviting her into his arm. As she accepted, he pulled her close, and she nestled into his neck. Peter sighed. Rebecca kissed his neck and inhaled deeply. He could immediately feel her body tense.

"You don't smell the same, Peter. What is it, perfume? Cologne?" She rolled away and onto her back. She spoke looking at the ceiling. "Is that why you've been home so late? You're fucking someone else?"

"Uh, I, uh, I..." He couldn't finish the sentence. He just lay there looking at his wife. Instinctively he knew she would never want to understand.

"What?" she persisted.

"I, I just, I just wanted to be touched." His words were drawn thin.

"With who?" Ice.

He froze and looked away from her eyes, "Well... with..." And the next word was framed by his lips but carried no breath or sound. He knew he had to tell her. If she found out through gossip in the small town, it would be the end of him. It might be the end now, but he had to try, he had to tell her.

"Who, Peter, who is she?" She was off the bed now, wrapping the sheet around her naked body. Trembling.

"Terrell," he whispered.

Rebecca didn't move. She was paralyzed.

Peter was up in the bed now, sitting on his heels. Begging her to understand.

She mouthed words, more to herself than to him. "Terrell?" An eternal second ticked by. "TERRELL? Oh my god, OH MY GOD." She began to scream. "I just don't understand. Have you always been gay? Has our whole marriage just been a lie? Am I not enough? Have I never been enough?" Her words tumbled out of her mouth, tripping over each other clumsily, crashing into vowels and consonants. Her agony clawed at Peter, tearing into him. The fishbowl he had been swimming in shattered into a million pieces, making it dangerous to walk on the floor, dangerous to move.

"We haven't slept together in months, Becky," he whispered. "It was..."

She cut in. "That's your reason? So sleep with another woman then."

"That would have been better? That would have been okay? I considered that too, if that makes it better."

"Well, maybe, no, I don't know. Oh Jesus, Peter." She turned and sat on the bed, her back to him.

"I'm not gay, Becky. I love you. Can't we talk? If not now, tomorrow? Let me explain?" He could feel her back shaking, her face in her hands, her sobs as he spoke. He was standing in water holding an electrical appliance.

She pushed words between her lips through tear-stained fingers. "But you were with a man."

"Yes, I was. I just wanted physical attention, affection."

"What's wrong with me?"

"Nothing, when you decide to be there." He lowered his head, expecting a blow. "You were never meant to find out." He knew she wasn't listening.

"You were with a man. You'll want a man again. How can I ever trust that you want to be with me first, how can I..." Her voice was barely audible.

"You're focusing on the five percent, not the ninety-five percent. The ninety-five percent is you, Beck. What we've built together."

"YOU CHEATED ON ME," she yelled, "WITH A MAN." She was hysterical.

There was a heavy silence in the room, punctuated by breathing and sobs of confusion and pain. The waiting hung like thick moss on cypress trees. Rebecca got up and walked into the bathroom, dragging the sheet behind her.

"Becky."

"You slept with a man, Pete. It wasn't just in your imagination. It wasn't porn on a private screen. I don't think I can ever get past that." And she closed the door, leaving him sitting in the middle of an icy, cold, empty bed.

In a flurry of time, Peter lost his wife, lost his friends, lost his life. Rebecca's desire to be accepted by Primrose Street was blinkered by fear, and slowly the fear matted all her thoughts together into a thick, waterlogged rope. In her need to find meaning inside her denial of what Peter was trying to show her, she had to destroy, and so she destroyed Peter as a father to his children. They refused to speak to him, his acts portrayed in the most gruesome way possible by their mother. His tongue was cut out, his five percent stretched so thin that it became invisible to him, his ninety-five percent blurred into blizzard conditions.

Before she finally left, she took a shovel to her garden, destroying all the root systems. She left Peter standing on the front porch as she walked out.

Invisible threads are being spun into webs between the trees, sticky webbing connecting leaves and tiny, delicate branches. The web begins to stretch from tree to tree, house to house. The web is imperceptible, but the trees feel its pull, almost a suffocation, a clouding of visions and intent. The strands of the web begin to extend, find their way inside cracks of houses. They weave around staircase spindles, bedposts on headboards, along dresser tops, and through hairbrush bristles. They pull on yearnings and longings and fears. It is a web that stretches thin and pulls to the point of breaking.

When Sofia first sells to Kevin, she doesn't realize he lives across the street from her. On their third encounter, she makes it clear that she does not sell out of her house. But she likes Kevin. She sees him playing with Merlin and Nicolas on the front lawn, Nicolas laughing that belly laugh as Kevin wrestles and tickles him, Merlin pulling on his shirt. She invites him in one day for lemonade, at Nicolas's pleading. He plays checkers with Nicolas and tells Sofia about his art. She says she wants to see some, and he looks up at her. His look shows surprise that anyone would be interested in him, in what he does. But he smiles a shy smile and goes back to checkers.

Kevin starts to babysit for Sofia, and they have lemonade days where he brings his art and talks with her. He tells her about working with Jina, who lives down the road. He talks a lot about Jina and how much she helps him. She finds out that Jina is a lawyer as well as an artist. Sofia knows that Kevin feels significant looking after Nicolas. She can see how he lights up when he talks about his art. And she knows he loves Nicolas.

She sees how they play games together, draw together, snuggle under a blanket together to watch TV. Sometimes he brings Paddy over so Merlin has a playmate too.

Of course, Kevin doesn't know that ever since Sofia heard that he has a lawyer for a friend, she has thought of nothing else. She thinks that maybe Jina can help her figure a way out. But she knows it is a slippery slope.

Nicolas is making some lemonade all over the kitchen counter and putting cookies on a plate. Jina and Kevin are coming to visit today. He loves his neighbours. He's hoping they can all play a game today, maybe Sorry, or build with his new Jenga blocks. Sofia has the newspaper spread out on the kitchen table and is searching the classifieds for jobs in Martineville. She knows it's time. She's known that for a long, long time.

ELEVEN PRIMROSE STREET: SOFIA

It was 2:00 a.m. The exchange of words had been mixed with alcohol around seven. The colour of the words had darkened like clouds on a horizon. Alcohol was running low as tempers began to heat up. It wasn't long before his response, seething through his teeth, was joined by a fist to the side or her head, knocking her to the floor. And yet it was she who was apologizing as she picked herself up off the floor. She heard Nicolas crying upstairs.

"I'm going to Nicolas. I need to see if he's okay."

Mike grabbed her arm.

"I'll be right back." She shook his arm free and went upstairs to Nicolas, hoping to settle him back to sleep. Sofia's heart sank as she climbed the stairs. Nicolas's bedtime stories always seemed to be loud voices of adults fighting downstairs. She worried about him. The damage she was doing to him by her poor choices. Nicolas's father had been a poor choice. In the beginning, it had been all smiles and flowers and making out at the back of the cinema. Then she got pregnant. She didn't even finish high school. Ralph wasn't going to let a baby and a woman ruin his plans. He was still going to college. So they all moved into a one-bedroom apartment together in the big city. Having a small baby meant Sofia just stayed at home. She did her best cooking and cleaning and looking after the baby. But she had no idea how. Not really.

Ralph was no help. He finished classes and went right to his job at the factory. When he came home, he was tired and wanted to sit and drink beer by the TV. Any conversation turned into a screaming match, and soon they were punctuated with violence. When he started staying out late and coming home smelling like a different perfume every night, Sofia packed up her bag, her baby, and walked out. Ralph didn't follow or try to find her. She stayed in women's shelters for a while, then a low-income housing apartment complex. Jobs were scarce with no high school diploma, and it was hard to make ends meet. She was often behind with her rent. Nicolas never had new clothes, and she couldn't remember the last time she wore shoes without holes in them. Fresh fruit and vegetables were things she'd look at longingly in the grocery store aisles. She had put a few apples in her pockets here and there, but for the most part they ate noodles out of a can for a dollar, mustard on white bread she could buy at the dollar stores, and water from the tap, when it worked. She had tried cat food a few times, just to have some meat. It wasn't the taste that put her off, more the realization that a cat down the road was having the same meal. She applied for jobs at McDonald's and Tim Hortons as a dishwasher, but competition was fierce, and often she didn't even get an interview. She was living off the thin amount that mother's allowance sent each month. She was getting desperate.

That was when she started selling drugs. She had considered selling her body but didn't know how that would work with small Nicolas in the next room. And she couldn't use hotel rooms; she had no childcare for Nicolas. So, when Martin approached her one day, she said yes. Martin was her slum landlord. He had never said too much when she couldn't pay rent, but she had watched what happened to other tenants, and she knew it wouldn't be long until she was next. He was offering her an out, and she was smart enough to know to take it. At first it felt so wrong, so sneaky, so dangerous. He had said she could sell to a different kind of buyer, younger women, even kids. He'd set up all the deals. All she had to do was deliver the goods and bring back the money. He would leave the goods in a paper bag in her recycle bin and tell her the drop details an hour before.

Her first drop was horrible. Nicolas was in the stroller. Martin liked that idea, but she didn't stop shaking for days. She handed over the paper bag, not knowing what was inside, not wanting to even look, and took an envelope, tucking it into the stroller. She didn't take a breath the whole way home. But nothing happened, and each time it got easier. She stopped shaking, she breathed easier, and her cheques got bigger and bigger. She could buy warm clothes for Nicolas and a new coat for herself. Nicolas had wrapped toys at Christmas and food that wasn't out of a cat food tin. She didn't have to steal fruit anymore, and her shoes were new and warm. She was able to move to a better apartment, out of the housing complex. Soon she began to dream. What she really wanted was to move out of the city, buy a house in a small town, and give Nicolas a normal life. She started to save.

Then she got comfortable and made a mistake. One drop, she looked at the buyer and smiled, tried to make conversation. He turned and walked away without taking her bag or giving her his envelope. Martin gave her a black eye and a fat lip. He told her next time he'd put her in the hospital. She considered going to the cops, but she really liked the new coat she just bought, light tan wool with a big hood trimmed with real fur. She decided she'd keep selling a little longer until she had enough for a small house. No more mistakes. When she looked at the map, Martineville was a small town not too far away by bus. She'd buy a house there just in time for Nicolas to start in kindergarten. She'd get her high school diploma and look for a real job.

Somehow, Martin got wind of her plans.

"Martineville, eh. Nice. Good plan. I ain't got too many people in that area. You can help more of them develop an ice cream habit, eh?"

"But I don't want to sell anymore, Martin. I want out."

"Ya want out. *Out*. Out ain't an option. But I'll get ya outta here at least. Leave it with me. I'll have a house for ya in a month. Move in the summer, and the kid can start in a new school."

She never imagined Martin would actually do it, buy the house and put her name on the deed. But here she was, Primrose Street in Martineville. The house was more than she could have dreamed of. Glassed-in front porch, fireplace in the living room/kitchen with a vaulted ceiling. A big living room and dining room. A big room for Nicolas furnished with a captain's bed and desk. And a newly decorated bedroom for her in soft green, with a brass bed furnished with pink and white porcelain globes. The bathroom had a Jacuzzi bathtub and a black granite stone countertop surrounding a drop-down white sink. The whole house was furnished, and there was food in the fridge. The backyard had a jungle gym, a treehouse, huge cedar trees, and a little flower garden with a small fountain in the centre. It was a dream. The price was high, though; more drops, more deals, bigger money. She was nervous. This was a much smaller town. It wouldn't take long for people to figure things out. She'd have to be so very careful. She had thought that Martin would somehow still provide her with the bags for the deals. But he said he had a contact, a partner who lived in Martineville. She'd be dealing with him now. His name was Mike. He was handsome, no doubt about it. He had charm. She was rather swept off her feet when he first came to the house to introduce himself. The first couple of deals were simple enough. Mike was efficient and expected the same of her. One deal had been a little bit delicate, he had told her, and she needed to massage things a little bit. But everything went smoothly, and when Mike came around he was surprised to see the envelope.

"This means a celebration. I thought we might lose this guy. Well done." He returned with a bottle of champagne and some Pepsi for Nicolas and a large pizza. They watched a Disney movie together, and Nicolas went happily to bed that night. Sofia was tired and was looking forward to an early night herself. But Mike had other ideas. He walked over to her and slid one arm around her waist and the other around her ass. Slowly, he put his mouth on hers. It had been a long time since Sofia had been with a man. She was caught between her voice saying this was a bad idea and the wetness between her legs. He had pushed her up against the kitchen counter, slid his hand under her shirt, and pulled hard on her nipples, kissing her mouth roughly. His other hand manoeuvred her out of her pants, unzipping his own and pulled her leg up around his waist, moving her onto him. She cried out as he entered her. Both his hands moved to hold her ass so he could pull her closer, fuck her hard as he came. He stood back after, zipped up, told her he hoped for more sales like this, and gave her ass a slap. "Next time I look forward to my cock in your mouth. Nice to have a money shot." He smiled and walked out the door. She stood there panting, her pants beside her feet. She thought she might vomit. That was a few months ago.

She finished singing to Nicolas as his eyes started to close, and she pulled the covers up, tucking him in. Ralph was a poor choice. She had made a lot of poor choices, but Nicolas was the best thing that had ever happened to her. He was her angel. Sometimes he was the only reason she didn't want to check out permanently. She kissed his forehead and pulled his door closed. She knew Mike was waiting downstairs. She took a deep breath as she came back into the kitchen. Mike was waiting impatiently. He was usually impatient.

Now she stood opposite him, putting the table between her and him.

"Nicolas is asleep. Please keep your voice down now."

Mike just looked down and began to speak. "Martin told you once before, and I'll tell you again, there is no out. You do a good job, and you'll keep doing a good job."

"Let's just keep it to the deals then, Mike." She spoke quietly, no emotion.

"That's what you say now, but I know you want it."

"Let's just stick to the transactions for a while." Mike didn't reply; he just walked out the door. She turned the lock behind him and shut off the lights. She needed a dog, a big dog. Merlin. She would name him Merlin the magician. Might slow Mike down, and she wouldn't feel the need to sleep on the floor in Nicolas's room anymore. She would start looking around tomorrow.

During the summer months, when rain is often withheld for weeks
at a time, the maples begin to wilt. They hang listlessly over the
sidewalks, their leaves shrivelled and withdrawn. As Mike walks along
Primrose Street, the maples hang heavily in his wake, even though it is
not a sultry summer evening. He is heading to Fourteen Primrose Street to
see his old high school chum Justin. He rings the doorbell. Kevin appears.

"Hi, your dad in?"

"DAAAAAD." Mike stands alone in the foyer. He hears low voices,
shuffling feet.

Justin appears through the kitchen archway. He slowly walks toward
his front door and extends his hand.

"Mike."

"Justin." They shake hands. "How you been?"

"Good. Good. Working hard."

"Yeah, I hear."

"You?"

"Working hard."

"Yeah, I hear too." Justin looks at his feet. "What ya need, Mike?"

"Sofia won't let me into her house, and now she has this big dog that
doesn't seem to like me much."

"Yeah."

"So, I was wondering if you might talk to her, ask her what's up.
See if she'll talk with me. I know she and Kevin talk."

"Mike, I really think that is your problem. It's not mine, and I'm not involving Kevin. Seriously. I've looked the other way with you selling to Kevin. I've looked the other way over a lot of things. But this is yours, Mike. All yours. Sorry, man."

"That's it?"

"I'm afraid so. Oh, I am officially asking you to stay away from Kevin. I want him to stop using, and you are not helping."

"He's been buying from Sofia, you know."

"No, Mike, he buys from you. And I want it to stop. Got it?" Mike purses his lips but says nothing. He is raging inside. "Take care, Mike." And Justin closes the door.

Mike stands for a moment facing the closed door. Then he turns and walks down the steps to the sidewalk.

He's fuming as he stands at the road beside the large maple, waiting for a car to pass before crossing the road and pounding on Sofia's door. But the car doesn't pass. It stops right in front of Mike, and the passenger window slides down. Mike leans into the car.

"Tabitha? What the fuck do you want?"

"Listen, the last thing I want is to talk to you, but as fate would have it you were standing there as I was driving by, and it saves me a trip."

"What the fuck are you jawing about?"

"Simply, Mike, it's done. You better get out of town before Jina and I press charges, and Dayna isn't far behind."

"What, she's driving behind you?" He laughs at himself. Pleased as punch by his wit.

"Wow. You really are a colossal asshole. No joke, Mike. I'm guessing Justin just told you to back off too. We're not protecting you. Don't pump your ego more than usual. We just don't want any more shit around here. And you're shit. So it's like this, leave or else. Surely even you can understand that." She doesn't wait for an answer. She rolls up the window, forcing him to stand back, and drives off, showering him with little stones.

"Bitch," he mutters as he crosses the street. It is hard to know who he is referring to.

EIGHT PRIMROSE STREET: MIKE

Mike stood inside Sofia's glass porch, outside the front door. He could hear the dog barking inside, saw the lights on, and knew the door was locked. No one was answering the doorbell. He had pushed it three times now. Clearly it was working, or the dog wouldn't be barking. This had been going on for a few weeks now. He knew he should just take what he wanted. He wasn't used to asking for sex, or for a job to be done, and he wasn't used to hearing No. He needed Sofia to get back to work. But she wasn't answering his calls or her door. He would have to resort to other measures very soon. He wasn't used to asking for anything more than once, if that. He didn't want Martin breathing down his neck because of this. Mike remembered being jilted by another little bitch, years ago, at his high school prom. He remembered finishing an exam and driving home in his beat-up blue Rambler, three on the tree.

He remembered walking through his front door and hearing his mom banging pots in the kitchen.

"So how'd the last exam go?"

"Pretty good, I think."

"Dinner is at six."

"Okay, then I'm going to prom."

"Oh, so you got a date. Who?"

"Sarah."

"Sarah. Haven't heard that name. Okay, well have fun. Last prom. Oh, before dinner can you go and pick your sister up at dance class?

She's finished in fifteen minutes. Oh, and Dayna needs a drive to work, you can drop her on your way."

Mike pursed his lips. His mother couldn't see through the walls. "I just got in the door."

"Well, go out again before getting settled."

"Jesus, Mom. I'm not a taxi."

"Watch your mouth and get going. It helps me out, Mike, surely you can do that." He was always picking up or dropping his sisters somewhere. Even his older sister couldn't seem to get anywhere alone. And there was girl stuff everywhere in the house. Often, he left the toilet seat up on purpose to remind them that there was a man in the house too. It was easier when his dad was around, then they all remembered there were men living there. His dad made sure of that. No one said no to his dad, not unless they wanted a bruise on the head. Especially Mike. Being the only boy, his dad expected certain things: no tears, no mercy. He would sometimes hear his mom crying at night while his dad told her over and over again that one woman wasn't enough. And no one could swear like his dad. He remembered his dad coming to one of his soccer matches. You could hear him from one end of the field to the other. They told him not to come back, but he came to every game. There was no one Mike wanted to emulate more. He was crushed when his dad left for good.

"Yep, sure, Mom. I'll go now," he said pleasantly but with a snarl on his lips. "Come on, Dayna, let's fucking go." He marched out the door and started the car. Dayna slid into the passenger seat and put on her seatbelt.

"Mom is wondering if you're staying here when school's done."

"No fucking way. What do you care anyway?"

"I don't really. I know you're a hot shot, but for me, you're an embarrassment. I hear what the girls say in the bathroom, the change room. Did you fuck everyone, Mike?"

He smiled. "Pretty much."

"Why do you have to be such a creep? And Mom just thinks the sun shines out of your ass. How do you do it?"

"Maybe I'm just like Dad, Dayna, ever thought of that?"

"More than once. Who you going to bang at prom this year? Oh wait, it's Sarah with the big tits."

"Fuck you, Dayna. Just shut up now, or you can walk to work." They drove the rest of the way in silence.

After dinner, Mike got dressed in his rented tux and headed off to pick up Sarah.

Her front door opened as he walked up the path and stood waiting for him.

"Wow, you look gorgeous," he said. Sarah blushed. Her burgundy satin gown was strapless, accentuating her tiny waist and large breasts. It fell to her feet. Her hair was curled and swept up on one side. She wore small silver earrings.

"Thanks, Mike." He offered her his arm and escorted her to his Rambler.

Mike reached across Sarah and opened the glove compartment, pulling out a pack of smokes. He opened the pack and pulled out a small joint. "It's only really enough for a few puffs, want some?"

"No thanks. Do you really want to start the night like this?"

"Yeah, I do. It just relaxes me." He lit up and dragged long and hard. He let out a big sigh. "Better." He flashed Sarah that dimpled smile, and she half smiled back. "I have something else if you prefer little pink pills."

"No, I'm good. Where do you get all this stuff?"

Mike kept this secret close to his chest. It was a small town, but he knew exactly what he'd be doing for money after high school. "Around," was his vague and standard answer.

The evening was a mix of swishing gowns, lush fabrics, tears, hugs, loud music, and the back seats of cars. All too quickly it was last song, and The Bee Gees were crooning a love ballad. Mike looked at Sarah and extended his hand. He wasn't very stable on his feet, having pulled on quite a few mickeys that evening on top of everything else, but she took his hand and they moved into the music together.

They leaned on each other as they made their way out of the gym, through the school doors to the parking lot. As they reached the car,

Mike slid his right hand around Sarah's waist and the other up to her neck, pulling her close to his face, and began to kiss her, and she gently responded. But he began kissing harder and harder, pushing his body against hers. She stopped and tensed. His tongue found her lips, then her teeth, and the hand on her waist slipped lower and started pulling her dress up, pushing her against the car. Sarah tried to take a step away and grab her dress, but he pulled harder.

"Mike, stop," she said. But now his tongue was in her mouth, and then he quickly swivelled her around so her stomach and hands were against the car, both his hands were pulling her dress.

Sarah twisted and screamed, "STOP... STOP." Mike had his hands up her dress now and was pushing hard against her, probing. He knew she wanted it. He laughed and whispered in her ear, pushing harder. Sarah was enraged. He was strong and held her tightly. She pushed back against the car and turned quickly around, punching him in the chest. It spurred him on.

"Come on, Sarah, you know you want to. I won't tell." He pushed against her, moving her legs apart with his feet.

"Fuck you, Mike." Her dress ripped as she tore away from him, tears streaming down her face, running across the parking lot. Mike's hand rested on the roof of the Rambler, his body leaning into the car door. He was breathing heavily, and things were slightly out of focus.

He slept in the back of his car in the parking lot that night. When he got home the next morning, the house was empty, and he gratefully slipped into his bed.

The dog barking brought him out of his reverie. He peeked through the lace curtains over the window and saw Sofia peering cautiously at the door from the kitchen. He laughed. A scowl spread across his face as he climbed into his Audi A8. He'd fuck her again, he thought, this time right on the kitchen table. Fast and hard, before she'd have time to protest. And then she'd do what she was told.

The thought comforted him as he started the ignition. He cranked up the tunes and wondered where Sarah was these days, and if she'd like a drive in his new black sports car. Besides, he thought, he hadn't really broken in these leather seats properly.

Dayna remembers Tabitha watching the squirrels play in her backyard, devouring the food in the feeders, when they were little girls. She liked to watch them hang upside down to eat. It was like watching Cirque de Soleil in the backyard. The birds were great, too, but they didn't put on the same kind of show. The maples were a great playground for the show. Dayna preferred the dance of the birds. It is a nice combo, Dayna and Tabitha.

They have been friends since grade two. They have weathered elementary school, high school, stayed in contact when they went off to college and university, and were maids of honour at each other's weddings. They had each other when often they felt like they didn't have anyone else.

Dayna never really connected with her brother Mike, even though there was only a couple of years between them, or her other sisters. She and Mike would always fight. Her sisters were older and busy. Mike was too handsome for his own good and slept with everyone in town. A chip off the old block, people would say. She and Tabitha would make bets as to who would be next, and if there was anyone left who hadn't been "Miked," as they called it. But it wasn't something Dayna laughed about.

Mike's last year of high school had been hard on Dayna. It was the year her dad finally walked out and the last year Mike would live at home. She was glad when her dad finally left. It had been agony with him around, loud, rude, and cruel to their mom. But he loved Mike. Everyone seemed to love Mike. Even though he was an ass, he could still help now and then. Dayna remembers the bird's nest in the maple tree one Saturday afternoon.

"It's going to fall and all the eggs are going to break," whined Dayna. She and Tabitha seemed intent on saving the nest.

"What the fuck is going on out here?" asked Mike. He got the long version from Dayna. "Relax. Who cares," he said.

"I care. Fine. I'll climb up and get it myself."

"Oh my fucking god. Just stay there." Mike left, came back with a ladder, leaned it up again the tree, and rescued the nest. He handed it to Dayna.

"Thanks, Mike," said Dayna, always shocked when he showed sensitivity.

"Sure. Now just shut the fuck up. I'm late now." He looked over at Tabitha as he walked to his car, but Dayna saw her just glare at him.

She remembers standing and looking at the speckled eggs inside the nest, wondering what they should do with it.

"Should we try to hatch them somehow?" Dayna asked her friend.

"Too late now," said Tabitha. "Besides, what would we do with them when they hatch? No, it's not a good idea. Sometimes it's best they just don't even come out of the egg. It would change our lives."

"Change our lives? Really, Tab. Maybe we should take them to biology class. See what Mr. Wozniak would do with them."

"No, he's creepy. Just flush them down the toilet. Just end it now, Dayna, just end it now."

Dayna looked at her friend with curiosity. "What's up with you?"

"Nothing, sorry. Bad day at school."

"Okay, forget the nest, I'll just put it in the bush beside the house."

"Sure. Then you can keep on eye on them, see if anything happens. There won't be any secrets that way."

Dayna raised her eyebrow and stared hard at Tabitha. She decided to not say anymore. "Hey, wanna get some ice cream?" she asked.

"Sure, ice cream helps everything," said Tabitha. "Yeah, ice cream helps everything," she repeated robotically.

"Okay, let's get us some." Dayna put her arm around her friend's shoulder as they started downtown.

FIFTEEN PRIMROSE STREET: TABITHA

There were three standing lamps around the table, about six inches high, like large, spherical stainless steel bowls approximately thirty-six inches in diameter, with bright bare bulbs inside. Six strips of fluorescent lighting hovered on the ceiling of corked white tiles, adorned with dots in various patterns. It wasn't a big room, maybe the size of a small kitchen. Along the back wall was a small sink and counter, spotlessly cleaned and clutter-free, an antibacterial soap dispenser waiting to the right side of the tap, half full of orange foaming cleanser. Glass-doored cupboards lined one wall, filled with sterilized empty jars, bottles of different sizes filled with different coloured liquids some with labels in foreign languages, bandages, gauze, metal objects, and packages, packages, packages. Emergency equipment for resuscitation of lungs and hearts was along the wall opposite the glass-doored cupboards. IV dispensers stood politely beside the resuscitation equipment. In one corner of the room was a large white machine that looked like a vacuum. It had a thinner suction tube attached to its flat top, curled like a snake in waiting on the top, and no writing anywhere on the canister.

The glare of the three bare bulbs reflected off the stainless steel tray beside a thin, long, tall table where Tabitha lay, goosebumps on her arms and down to her belly, a thin paper-green gown barely covering her body. The stainless steel tray held instruments: razor-thin steel knives of different sizes, plastic tubes, transparent rubber gloves, various sizes of needles and matching syringes, gauze patches and rolls, white tubes, thick elastic bands, small bottles of colourless liquids.

She lay on the long, tall, steel table in her paper-thin green gown, waiting. She was cold. Her eyes had been occupied counting the dots beside the fluorescent bulbs on the ceiling. Three nurses were shuffling around the room, moving metal objects that would clink together, opening and closing the glass-doored cupboards, washing things in the sink and whispering to each other. She let the nurse-noise become part of the pattern the dots made on the ceiling.

"Wear a light, loose-fitting summer dress," she remembered the lady saying on the phone. "You need to be here by 10:00 a.m., and you'll be out around four. Make sure you have a driver to take you home."

Mike had said he'd drive her, but he was irritated by the situation, as he put it.

"Weren't you on the pill?" was the first question he asked.

"Odd time to ask that question," she replied.

"Well, were you?" he persisted.

"No, Mike. You knew that. You said you had a condom. Or maybe you were more drunk than you realized."

"Well, it was a pretty big party."

"So, did you use a condom?"

"Were you on the pill?"

"Did you use a condom?" Her voice was getting more loud and shrill.

"Well, I GUESS NOT, TABITHA," he offered obnoxiously.

They stood in awkward, heated, pregnant silence.

"Let's not advertise this, okay?" he directed.

"No, we wouldn't want to smear your reputation now, would we Mike," she virtually spat at him. "I can't very well start university pregnant. I don't think I could ever go home again. Fuck, it would certainly make Maggie's day."

"Jesus, just leave your fucking family out of this for one minute."

"What about your sister? She'd kill you. She's my best friend."

"Tabitha, let's just put it down to alcohol and hormones and leave it at that. Jesus, what a fucking mess. What are the dates again? Why can't you just go to the hospital in town?"

"Fine. I don't want to hear it all again." He drove her.

It was a tense and quiet drive to Buffalo. Mike didn't really know the way and lost his temper with her inability to read a map. He broke the turn signal arm right off the steering column. Tabitha sat in silence looking down as he kicked the broken turn signal behind his feet. Trees moved by the car too quickly. She looked back, her gaze lingering on their soft, forgiving branches as one looks out of a train window at the person left on the platform. Maybe they were looking at her, trapped in a cage racing ahead, while they disappeared like dots into the distance.

It was a long drive, so they decided to leave the day before and stay in a hotel close to the clinic. It had sharp angles of concrete designed into its 1980s-style exterior, taupe that made no significant statement as they walked into the foyer, pale ceramic floor tiles in a limp lobby. There were few plants, no gardens or water fountains. Sterile, leafless arrangements of sticks and artificial flowers stood in wide, clear urns approaching the check-in counter. Tabitha noticed one vase of fresh-picked stargazer lilies on the desk of the concierge. She went over and slowly began tracing her finger around the orange/white petals, stamen stain bleeding into her fingertips. She rubbed her fingertips together, watching the stain spread, careful not to wipe it on her light pale-yellow cotton summer dress. She'd never get that stain out. Mike was hailing her, waving keys. They settled into the space, and Mike ordered room service.

The meal arrived on a table with white linen, hanging down low enough to cover the wheels on the table. A wine bottle sat on an angle in the stainless steel bucket, filled with ice. Stainless steel meal covers reflected the light in the room, teasing with delicious aromas of spice and herbs and shellfish. The waiter accepted his tip and left the room. They ate in silence, his plate quickly empty, her plate more than half full.

"Hey," he joked with her, "wanna have sex? We won't need a condom or a pill."

Tabitha went to have a bath.

"Miss?" She turned from dot #73 she was counting on the ceiling, making a note of where it was in relation to the bulbs, and turned her face in the direction of the nurse. "We need your watch off, and if you would just slide down a bit farther to the end of the table. The doctor is almost ready."

She slid down, obediently, the green-paper gown clumping in folds around her hips. She clicked off her watch, handed it to the nurse, and went back to dot 73.

She hadn't told anyone. No one needed to know; it would have been distorted by the morning gossip anyway. She wasn't sure her friends would look at her the same way after; no point in taking a chance. Where would she start anyway? She especially couldn't tell her family. And never ever her dad. She so wished she could tell Dayna. They'd never had secrets from each other. But somehow she didn't know how. Not this time.

When she'd suggested adoption as a possibility to Mike, he had only said, "Then everyone will know." Anyway, she'd have a hard time starting university pregnant as a single mother.

Her doctor kept saying it was her choice, her body, as he filled in his report... he didn't even mention keeping "it," he didn't suggest anyone to talk to before making her decision. He couldn't approve her for the procedure here, but he did give her the name and number of a clinic in Buffalo. When she called they would tell her the fee, and it would just be a day treatment. She would need a driver. "But time is a factor here; their fee increases each day after eight weeks of fetal growth." Other family planning clinics were closed for the summer or were short-staffed. She decided to take the doctor's suggestion. Mike said he'd cover the cost after a lot of arguing.

The three nurses were moving more quickly now. The doctor shuffled into the room, the only male in the building, tall, mid-thirties, white coat, black hair, wire-rimmed glasses. He wheeled the vacuum from the corner, parking it at the end of the table, moving a stool to the end of the table where she lay. He picked up a large syringe from the stainless steel tray, loading it with a clear liquid... looking at no one, speaking to no one. The nurse standing beside the doctor was talking. "Miss, put your feet in the stirrups and slide down more."

The second nurse was moving things around on the stainless steel tray, the noise of steel connecting with steel was echoing off the white walls and bowled lamps. To Tabitha it sounded like cymbals being crashed together.

The third nurse picked up the young woman's hand. "Won't be long now. You'll just feel a little prick." Tabitha turned her face from counting dot number 91 on the ceiling to look at the nurse who had spoken, not understanding what she had said but feeling an odd sensation on the inside of her thighs and then around her vulva... involuntarily she squeezed the nurse's hand harder, tears stinging into her eyes, her knees struggling together but prevented from moving by the rubber-gloved hands of the nurse beside the tray as the freezing needle pierced the skin deep in her vagina again, and again.

92, 93, 94...

The doctor was sitting on the stool now, disconnected, moving her soft, private, intimate labia and cervix like pages of a text being studied for an exam and probing deeper with the needle.

95, 96, 97...

She thought of the evergreen trees in her backyard. Their needles could be soft as they lay bedding the ground, but a wrong step could bring out a sliver of blood from her bare feet; they could be sharp as sewing needles. But their fragrance spoke of waiting, listening, being... and she would sometimes lie down on those needles and look up as the evergreens towering above her, tall and thin and arching ever so slightly...

98, 99...

"It'll just be a minute now," the doctor said, really to himself, as he turned his attention to the vacuum beside him now. The nurse released Tabitha's knees, letting them fall together. Tabitha couldn't remember when she'd last taken a breath. The other nurse began to release her hand, but Tabitha held it tighter, like she'd hold a branch when climbing into a tree, careful not to slip and fall. She could feel a thin layer of perspiration on her face and neck, spreading onto her chest and heat across her cheeks. Trails of tears ran from the corners of her eyes down to behind her ears.

101, 102, 103, 104...

The nurse had moved the tray and was standing beside the doctor now, handing him instruments. The other nurse had pulled the reluctant knees apart again, her rubber-gloved hands staying firmly in place.

The young woman's hand tightened on the hand inside hers. "Just try to relax, you won't feel a thing," a voice was saying.

Someone had switched on the vacuum. Would there be such a mess on the floor afterward? She felt her pubic hairs being pulled up, and with a sickening knot gripping deep in her belly and rising up as vomit in her throat, she realized the small white tube-like probe from the stainless steel tray was now on the end of the small vacuum hose and was being inserted inside her vagina… they were sucking her life out with a vacuum. Her eyes closed, heavily.

Her cells were paralyzed as she strained to leap off the table, to scream, to run, but like an animal caught in the blaze of headlamps on a road, she couldn't move. The snare just shattered what was inside its teeth and outside its steel.

Tear tracks wore into the sides of her face.

104, 105, 106…

It wasn't a pain, like slicing into your skin with a blade; it was more like a pressing ache beginning in one spot and reaching and moving and grabbing until it consumed everything inside… she felt the ache splinter through her body like an axe, slowly and deliberately chopping wedges into a tree's flesh until there was nothing but wood chips and slices and the emptiness of a tree falling, falling, through space.

107, 108, 109…

Her hand had been put back onto the edge of the table, alone, exposed, naked… the vacuum was wheeled back into the corner, the probe disconnected and dropped loudly onto the tray, the small hose wiped clean and folded neatly on top of the white, wordless machine. The contents of the tray crashed into the hollowness of the stainless steel sink at the back of the room, her already tense assaulted body quivered with the cacophony of sound. The dots blurred on the ceiling as she felt something move along her inner thighs and her hips being lifted slightly. And then there was a soft, thick wad between her legs, snugged up against her swollen labia, and a strap around her waist. She was being made to move off the table, the green gown clumped to one side. She yearned to crawl on her hands and knees across the floor, into a dark corner. She was led into the adjoining room.

It was small and dark. The walls were a dark kind of green, and there was one dim bulb on the ceiling, covered by an opaque brown glass light fixture. Seven army-type cots, in random design on the floor, filled the room, small bodies were curled into balls on each cot; no empty cots, no signs of life… like a raped rainforest with only stumps remaining. An Emily Carr painting she'd seen once.

There were no sounds except for the nurses cleaning in the other room, setting the next trap, and the hum of the air conditioner struggling on the wall to keep things cool. The only other object in the room was a small sink in the corner.

She watched the doctor out of the corner of her eye as she gingerly lay on her side on the narrow cot, a thin grey blanket carelessly draped over her body, not quite resting on her shoulder, goosebumps covering her entire body now. She watched, only her eyes moving, as he hunched his lanky, tall body over the tiny sink, aimlessly pushing the plunger on the large bottle of green disinfectant soap on a ledge above over and over again, filling the palm of one hand with the liquid, one strand of hair hanging randomly over his left eye, just to the side of his wire-rimmed glasses. His white jacket was bloodstained and tight across his shoulders. He was ardently and intently washing his hands. Around and over and under, around and over and under he moved the green soap into all crevices and creases in his hands, and the water and soap began to dilute the blood. She watched as the thick, dark blood became lost and colourless as the water swirled it, carried it, down the drain.

She closed her eyes, listening to the water, imagining herself sliding down the drain with the diluted blood, down into a stream. And there, buoyed by the water, she rolled onto her back and was gently moved along the river by rocks and currents. The burbling sounds of the water were comforting. She blinked the water from her eyelids and saw leaves overhead, and weeping branches stroking down to the surface of the water, running their tips into the liquid like a distracted canoeist's paddle, she imagined back of her hand skimming the water as the boat moved along. She closed her eyes again, still on her side on the hard cot but lulled by the sound of the water, comforted by the maples. A tear slipped out from under her left eyelid, quickly finding the worn groove, trickling over the temple, pooling around her ear and seeping into the worn, flat pillow. Another tear collected in the corner of her closed right eye. The thin grey blanket fell completely away from her, leaving her shoulder exposed and cold. But she didn't move; the cold was comforting, distracting. Her eyes stayed closed as she drifted downriver into cool pools and a numbing sleep.

Robert looks right through the trees outside his house and along the street. His only goal is to get the teeth of his chainsaw firmly embedded into any tree limb and hack it off. He is the only person on Primrose Street who owns a chainsaw. Everyone else leaves the pruning of trees to the city. Any trees in backyards are so small, a handsaw would do the trick if trimming was needed. But Robert likes things done his way. He always says it takes too long for the city to even call him back, let alone deal with a situation. So he takes matters into his own hands with his own chainsaw. The whining buzz can be heard all down the street, as can Robert's impatient, loud voice as he yells at his son, Derek, who is reluctant to use the chainsaw himself. Derek is only ten years old. The chainsaw weighs almost as much as he does. He looks imploringly through the window into his house, where his mother, Cheryl, hides. She is cowering in the kitchen, never knowing what to do. The choice between unleashing more of Robert's anger as a result of protecting her boy is a hard one for Cheryl. Derek knows she can see him.

Robert doesn't like the maple tree at the front of his house, but he knows it is on city property, so he can't really touch it. That doesn't stop him from trimming the limbs that hang over into his yard. Well, "trim" is the politically correct word he would use; in fact, Robert butchers everything he touches with that chainsaw. Cheryl hates how he saws off limbs and just leaves the tree in tatters. Derek stands without blinking.

"Here are a few lower branches just waiting for you, son. Bring over that chainsaw." Derek fights back tears as he lugs the chainsaw over to his dad.

"Okay, now pull that cord as hard as you can."

"I don't want to, Dad."

"That is not the answer, boy. You need to learn to do his. Now pull the cord." Derek pulls and pulls, but he just isn't strong enough to get it started. His dad starts cursing and strides over, snatching the chainsaw from his hands and pulling the ripcord until it purrs.

"Okay, you can't start it, but let's see you hold the trigger and cut off these lower branches." Derek is ready to throw up. He reaches over and touches the bark of the tree, feeling a quiver and not sure if it is his own or the tree's. But the choice of throwing up or meeting with his dad's temper is a no-brainer. He swallows hard, feeling small chunks fight their way back down his throat, lifts the chainsaw over his head, and tries his best to saw off a limb. The chainsaw slips in his hand, barely missing his foot as it hits the ground. He stands there panting and crying.

"Jesus Christ, Derek. What the fuck. Fine, I'll just do it myself. At least sit there and watch." Derek sits perfectly still, hardly breathing. He never breathes much when he is around his dad.

"Robert, can't you leave some branches?" Cheryl pleads through the screened window. "It nice to have some shade in the yard, and the kids like to hang bird feeders from them."

"What are you fucking talking about? Shade. Bird feeders. What the fuck. Are we starting a bird sanctuary now?" And he ends the almost conversation with his wife as he revs his chainsaw and lops off the tree's branches, leaving a few leaves on the top and a stump below.

"There." He drops the chainsaw beside Derek, still whirring. "Shut if off and put it in the garage. And bring me a beer from the fridge in there."

When Robert isn't sawing wood, he is in the truck, his hunting guns beside him on his way out of the city. Derek accompanies him, having little to no say in the matter. He hates hunting more than the chainsaw and cries whenever his dad kills. Amanda offers to go instead of Derek. But Robert says it is no place for a girl, so she stays home.

"Why don't you go on your own today, Robert?" Cheryl suggests. "I'd like Derek to help me with a few things today."

"Baking? That'll sissy him up a bit more. No, he can come with me." And so he does. Cheryl packs them a lunch and puts some bottles of water and Coke in the truck. She kisses Derek goodbye, says it will be okay, knowing it won't be at all. Robert will talk at Derek for the whole trip, and Derek will feel like icicles have invaded his stomach. They will tromp through the bush; his father will thrust a large rifle into his hands. He'll show him all the right ways to shoot a gun and then put a mark on a tree. It's always the same.

"There, come on now, a girl could hit that mark. And once you do that, a deer is next." Derek will choke back tears as he pulls the trigger and will find himself flying through the air and landing on his backside in the dirt. His father will pick him up by the shirt, plop him on his feet, and do it all over again. Only when he sees a deer or a pheasant in the distance will he take the gun himself, shoot for the kill, and say it is time to call it a day. As much as Derek hates to see something die, he finds himself praying for wildlife to come close by so he can stop shooting practice. There will be icy silence in the truck on the way home, broken by more insults about how Derek needs to toughen up, man up with a gun.

"Next time, boy, you are shooting that deer." Derek prays there will never be a next time. He longs for the day he will be big enough to stand up to his dad. When they get home, Derek leaps out of the truck and runs to his room, closes the door, and buries his head in his pillow so no one can hear his sobs, least of all his father. Amanda will gingerly tiptoe into his room, bringing colouring books and snacks. They'll sit on the floor together and work on the pages. Derek loves his sister. She always knows what to do. She is seven years old.

TWENTY-EIGHT PRIMROSE STREET: DEREK

He remembered the moment like accidental imprints in newly poured concrete. The moment when DeeDee kissed Mark for the first time.

He had accepted admission to a college miles and miles away from home, in another province where he was a complete stranger. From the first day on campus, he'd dressed in androgynous fashions to keep his gender a mystery. It felt freeing and terrifying all at the same time. He called himself DeeDee. His voice had never been particularly low, so that wasn't an issue. He wore his hair cropped short, with stylish, silver, loopy earrings in both ears, hints of makeup. Breasts were the biggest problem; he didn't have them. So he wore very baggy shirts instead, shirts that came below his hips and covered his crotch. Luckily, he wasn't well endowed in any significant area. He borrowed the baggy look from a neighbour back home, Mrs. Miller's daughter Sylvia. She loved big, baggy shirts, although in her case it was to hide her very large breasts. Packaging was purposeful, whatever the product inside. He had experimented with bras because he couldn't wear baggy clothes all the time. He tried various styles of bras and various materials to fill out the cups. A push-up bra seemed best, and paper towels became the voluptuous inside. His illusion was convincing, even to him. His biggest hurdle was public bathrooms. If he were ever to walk into a men's washroom, the illusion would be shattered and he'd risk broken bones, and if he was caught in a ladies' restroom he could be arrested. He opted for the jail possibility. Choice was very limited in this world of illusion and disguise. Costumes and masks. He had been wearing a costume his whole life. It was time to take it off.

He lived by himself off campus. It helped him adjust and get used to living outside the lines drawn early in his youth by others, especially his father. He remembered playing dress-up with his sister when they were three and four years old. Everyone laughed, said it was normal and they didn't know better. He'd been ten years old when he first put on his sister's dress. His dad was at work that Saturday afternoon, his mother, Cheryl, and sister Amanda were at a birthday party down the road. He'd said he'd be fine alone, happy to play video games. And he had been fine, so fine as he smoothed the yellow summer dress with blue polka dots down at the sides and adjusted the V-neckline. Fine as he felt normal for once. Fine as she turned and watched herself in the mirror, seeing the dress dance around her, swing and sway. Fine as she felt herself come to the surface, like she was finally really looking at herself in the mirror. Smiling, beaming. So very fine as she turned to look at the back of the dress in the mirror, and then she heard it, the door creak, and there was the reflection of his father in the glass standing beside the sweet, happy girl in the mirror. He froze. Robert was home unexpectedly early, grim and looming in the door frame to Amanda's room.

It took two strides for the big man to cross the room, grab Derek by the arm, rip the dress from his body, break his nose, crack a rib, and break his arm as he hit the floor, unconscious. It took two hours until he was taken to the hospital, because Robert just left him on the floor until his mother came home after the party; two days he stayed in a private hospital room so no one would be able to hear the real story; two years to learn how to colour inside his father's lines, which meant finally killing a deer on a hunting trip and preparing it for the freezer; six more years to learn to wear his costume effectively, convincingly.

Now, at university, it was his colouring book, and the pages had no lines at all.

He'd seen Mark before on campus; in classes, at the library. Each time, he'd get a quivery feeling in his gut and would feel his cheeks flush red and hot. A feeling he'd never allowed himself before. They began to talk after class, walk to and from classes together. He liked how he laughed. How he moved. He imagined what it would be like to hold his hand, kiss him, tell him the truth. To finally let DeeDee be free, be loved, be her. Not him. Not Derek. Derek was an actor in a play. And then it happened, Mark asked DeeDee out on a date. There was a band playing at the local pub, and Mark asked if she wanted to go.

There she was, DeeDee, sitting on a bar stool, talking to Mark, flirting instinctively, wearing a long-sleeved dark blue dress with a soft, round neckline and a silver necklace dangling a small bird in flight, silver hoops hanging from her ears. She wore two silver rings and a thin watch on her left wrist. She was drinking a strawberry daiquiri, he was having a rum and coke. DeeDee noticed how his mouth moved when he laughed. How his jeans clung to his muscular legs, how his pale blue-collar shirt had two buttons undone at the top. She imagined his chest underneath. Mark laughed, and DeeDee's red lips slowly opened into their own laughter, blushed cheeks lifting, earrings swinging.

"Wasn't it just crazy how he went on and on not even knowing?" laughed Mark.

"Well, really, someone should have told him, don't you think?"

"Yeah, I guess. But when a prof walks around with toilet paper trailing from his shoe, well, you have to get something out of it." They laughed and sipped their drinks.

"You made a great comment the other day," said Mark.

"Really?"

"Yes, you know. About how colour has frequencies, and that's why we like wearing certain colours on certain days. You doing your paper on that?"

"I am, I am. Thanks." DeeDee was swirling in emotion.

"What's your major anyway?"

"Arts. I want to do work in graphic art one day."

"Cool. Well, I'm glad you're in my psych class."

"Yeah, me too." DeeDee had tingles all over her body.

"Do you want another drink?"

"Sure, that would be great. So what are you majoring in?"

"Political studies for now. But I don't know really. I'll see."

"I took a political class. Really liked it. Made me wonder if I should change or combine my major."

"Art and politics. Could work." They listened to the band, sipping their drinks.

"You like the band? Do you want to dance?" DeeDee froze.

"Yeah, I'd love to, but I'm really loving talking to you right now. And the daiquiri's great." She was terrified that anything below her waist would brush against him.

"Sure. No problem. Where are you from?" And the conversation drifted in and out of the noise behind the bar, the people on the dance floor, the music of the band until in a suspended moment, Mark leaned over and kissed DeeDee on her red lips. Soft, lingering, longing inside yearning. DeeDee held her breath, lost in the glory of the moment, until she felt Mark's hand begin to slide up her thigh and under the hem of her dress. DeeDee sat back, crossed her legs, reached for her drink, as casually as humanly possible.

"Sorry," said Mark with affection, "too fast?"

"Yeah," whispered DeeDee, eyes down so Mark could not see the tears welling up. Now the music was deafening, and she felt paralyzed.

It could never happen. Mark's hand could never finish that journey up her thigh. And DeeDee could never enjoy it as she wanted to, needed to, yearned to. How could she ever have "that" conversation with him. It would be like asking the sea to be rid of all its salt. DeeDee was caught in a web of illusion and despair. Sticky, tangled. She could see no way out. She had no one to talk to. She would just end up in another strand of the web. She wanted to be bound and so consumed by the spider. Anything would be easier than this. She felt like water left running into a tall glass, flowing over the edge, swirling down and out of sight.

Derek went home for Thanksgiving. He kissed his mother hello and hugged her a little longer.

"I didn't think you were coming, honey, such a great surprise. And guess what, Dad just left for his hunt. You just missed him."

"Well, that was a bit of luck." And he laughed like a plant not watered in weeks.

"I have all your favourites, I made them just in case." She hugged him again.

"Hey, look who's here." Amanda came over and hugged her brother. "How's school?"

"The art program is really fantastic, and I've met some great people. What about you? Haven't had a text in a bit from you."

"She has…" began her mother. "Right, sorry, honey. Go ahead."

"Anyway, I'm sorry I haven't been texting or emailing. I'm officially doing my last internship at the hospital in town here, which makes it much easier to get a job here. And Evan and I are getting pretty serious." She blushed.

"That's great, just so great. I love you."

Derek smiled at his sister and hugged her again.

"Grandma's coming to dinner too, Derek," said Cheryl.

"Oh, good. Hopefully Dad won't be home in time for dinner, and we can have a nice Thanksgiving for a change." No one responded. They all just busied their hands.

"Derek, honey, will you set the table? You always do such a nice job."

"Sure, Mom." He started to collect the placemats and napkins. His mother came over and stroked his arm.

"I'm really glad you came home, Derek."

"Yes, me too."

"Are you finding some friends at college? Are your courses going well?"

"Yeah, some friends. Courses are going well."

"Derek, seriously, why did you not go to Toronto on that scholarship?" asked Amanda.

"Really? Think I would have ever heard the end of that?"

"But you're still in the arts out east. Who cares what he thinks?"

"Everyone, it seems." And he continued setting the table. Amanda came up behind him.

"He makes it hard for everyone, Derek."

"Come on, it's not the same and you know it. "

Amanda knew he was right. "Well, I love you, Derek." She hugged him again.

"Well, you're the only one. I'll get the rest of the plates." She stood there, sadly watching him walk away. Not knowing what to do or what to think.

Dinner filled the table, and things were light and happy until Robert came in late with a few too many beers showing on his face.

"Well, look who decided to show up after all." And he slapped Derek hard on the back, sending his fork across the table and out of his hand.

"Robert," said Cheryl, "just wash up and sit down."

"Come on, Dad, we set a plate for you. Sit here beside me," said Amanda, feeling the chill settle over the table.

"I don't need to wash up. I'm good. Pass the plate of turkey, Cheryl. I'm starved. And after dinner, we have some pheasants to clean, boy. It was a great day in the bush."

After dinner, and before cleaning pheasants with his dad, Derek went to his room. He took his backpack and some equipment from his dad's cabinet. It wasn't a large bedroom, big enough for a desk, a chair, a double bed, and space to walk between furniture. There was a window over the desk, a closet. He sat on his bed with his back to the wall and looked at the posters he had put up in high school. Van Gogh's *Starry Night*. Michael Phelps in his bathing suit after the Olympics.

Derek sighed. He would never fit. He belonged nowhere. He reached over into his backpack and put the letter on his desk, then picked up his dad's small handgun, loaded it, put the barrel carefully into his mouth, closed his eyes, and pulled the trigger. A little bit of blood had dripped off the wall and onto the cream-coloured comforter. That stain would be permanent.

Kevin finds a small new maple tree growing in a corner of his front yard while raking the leaves the afternoon of Derek's funeral. It is small and fragile, not strong enough to stand up to a pile of leaves. It has five full delicate, soft leaves already, soft as a newborn's palm, a new bud breathed into being. Even though they are red and orange and soon to fall off, they have a feeling of newness.

It is a dull grey fall day. Kevin has been watching people moving to the church all morning. He's pretty sure the whole town will be there. He's also pretty sure there will be protesters. He read the signs as people walked by: suicide doesn't belong in church, God punishes sin. He stopped reading after the second one and raked with more vigour, keeping his eyes down.

He is a few years younger than Derek. They often spoke when they were younger, playing on the street. Derek and Kevin were two of the few boys who didn't play road hockey in the summer or ice hockey in the fall. It is tough being a boy and living in a town in Ontario, not playing hockey. Teasing starts early at school. Kevin felt the sting of that bullying day after day. He couldn't imagine what Derek went through, especially if anyone really knew. He kept it all a pretty good secret. But to be trapped in the wrong body and have a father like Robert, Kevin feels heavy in his heart. He realizes he has it pretty good. He is doing okay at school. His art is being appreciated by Jina, and he is starting to believe he could actually have a career doing what he loves. He is making new friends. His dad is amazing. It's pretty good. Especially when he thinks of Derek down the road in a pine box.

He finishes raking the one side of the garden and moves over to the part closer to the sidewalk. He can hear the bells at the church beginning to ring. He imagines Derek lying prim and proper in his coffin at the front of the sanctuary. Kevin would hate people looking at him like that. And there will be hundreds of people there. He knows he will hear the singing from his front lawn. He thinks of Amanda. She was always very protective of her brother. He sees her in his mind sitting in the front pew, tears staining her face as she has to watch all the people gawk at her brother. He keeps raking.

"Hey, Kev."

"Hey, Nicolas." He drops the rake just in time for Nicolas to run and jump up, wrapping his legs around Kevin's waist and giving him a big hug. Sofia walks up behind him. She has a tired smile on her face.

"Hey, Kevin. You not going to the funeral today? You can walk with us if you like."

"Nah, I can't do those things. And there's way too many people there."

"Yeah, that's for sure. I hear almost everyone will be there."

"Well, not me. I'm raking."

"Did you hear that his dad is coming to the funeral? They say he looks pretty thin and drawn."

"I sure hope the fuck he does. Sorry, Nic." He picks up the rake.

"Want to come over for milk and cookies when we get back?" asks Sofia.

"Yeah, I'd like that."

"Okay, Nicolas will come and get you."

"Yeah, and be ready to play a game, Kev."

"I sure will, little man. See ya, guys."

Kevin finishes raking and goes back into the house. He doesn't want to hear the bells anymore. He has told his dad he isn't going, so he has the house to himself. His thoughts drift back to Amanda and her mom. Even though there will be so many people there today, he has a sense they will be feeling really, really alone.

He decides to do something for Derek. He goes and gets his large sketchbook, pastels, and charcoal pencils. Then he digs around in his drawer and finds a photo of him and Derek one summer when they went fishing. Kevin was pretty little, so they just had rocks tied to the end of a rope tied to the end of a stick, and they'd drop it in the water. They really weren't catching anything; they just liked the sound of the rock plopping into the water. But they told everyone they'd gone fishing. His mom had taken a picture of them when they returned. Two cherubs beaming like they've just caught the Big One.

He remembers how much Derek loved the big maple tree in his front yard too. He had a little bird feeder he had hung on one of the branches for the winter cardinals. He loved their bright red colour. It was one of his favourite colours. His dad took his chainsaw to those branches. But Kevin can see still see it in his mind's eye. And so he begins to draw and shade and create a piece of art where Derek is hanging the bird feeder on the maple's big broad branch, a cardinal waiting in the top boughs. And he uses the fishing photograph to get Derek's face just right.

He'd like to get Jina's thoughts before taking it over to Derek's sister. Jina invited him in for tea one day, and he saw her paintings. They were awesome. That's when he started talking about his art. He's learned a lot from Jina. Kevin doesn't know why she's a lawyer and not an artist full-time. He'll ask her someday. Meanwhile, he wants to do a great job on this piece for Derek. The bells have stopped ringing. They'll be talking about Derek now. He traces his finger around Derek's face in the picture, remembering their fishing trip. Remembering the cardinal. He pulls out the red chalk pastel and starts creating.

He'll take the bus over to where Jina works tomorrow and show her the piece.

TWENTY-THREE PRIMROSE STREET: JINA

They're supposed to come every twenty minutes, Jina thought to herself. She had already been waiting for half an hour. The bus schedule was more like one every hour and twenty minutes, or whenever they felt like showing up. What was really irritating was riding the bus to an important meeting. You depended on that bus to get you there on time. That's when the driver decided to pull over at the donut shop. It wasn't any special time, like lunch or mid-morning coffee, nothing like that. These stops had no real pattern. Maybe it wasn't coffee and donuts he stopped for. Jina glanced at her wristwatch, a thin gold band with a round face and points in place of the numbers. An old-school kind of watch. It was already 7:25 p.m. and it was cold. It never seemed to matter how many layers she had on; when she stood on the curb waiting for a bus, she froze.

Damn bus. It was dark, too. It made her a little nervous walking home at night, especially when the avenue had only one or two streetlights. There wasn't a whole lot in Jina's fridge, which was unfortunate because she was starving. She usually had a couple of granola bars in her briefcase for these occasions, but she hadn't replenished in a while. Her fingers discovered a piece of chewing gum in a corner of the pocket on her coat... Juicy Fruit, the long piece with the silver foil wrapping covered in yellow paper. That should keep the juices flowing until she got home and could order some takeout. Now 7:35 and still no bus — wait — it just rounded the corner. Her fingers were starting to freeze around the handle of her briefcase.

The bus pulled to a stop, and she climbed the steps, fumbling with her gloves and frozen fingers to open the bus pass for inspection. Her car seemed to be in the shop a lot lately, so she decided to get a pass. She hated the bus. The driver's name was on a little wooden sign above his head, over the window: Nathan Bosch. Jina gave him a quick eye. She navigated toward a seat in the middle of the bus, near the window; less chance of getting nauseous there. Jina really didn't like riding the bus at all. She settled in. Jina always settled in, took off her gloves, ran her fingers through her long, black hair. She wished she had remembered her hat. She also wished she had remembered some food. But tomorrow was shopping day. She would pick up some oranges; she needed the vitamin C. She loved squeezing the oranges; they reminded her of Lucy.

Lucy had such wonderful breasts, much like the size of a good orange and just as succulent. Jina remembered how she could tease her nipple with her tongue until Lucy squirmed a little. The men at the grocery store usually gave her an uneasy sideways glance as they put their very soft oranges into their baskets, not knowing that she was thinking exactly the same thing. Standing by the orange bin could be inspirational. She saw her next work of art as abstract: a woman sampling a large orange, the juice dripping down her shirt and pooling around her nipples, leaving wet spots on the shirt. She laughed softly to herself. She really must be tired to be thinking this way. The cold, the bus, needing food and the late hour had strange effects on people, especially Jina.

Jina was a good artist. She had dabbled in the arts since she was young. She wanted to be an artist and was always surprised to find herself carrying a briefcase. Her wardrobe was conservative but chic, not dowdy, but not artistic — unlike her colleague at the law firm where she worked. Tabitha always dressed like a fashion magazine. Her life was so easy. Great kids, daughter of the boss. Jina had tried to stand apart from Tabitha by dressing alternatively... wearing Indian-print cotton dresses, long, baggy sweaters with tights underneath, purple boots to her knee, green shirts with high collars that glowed in the dark, black lipstick. She even had a purple streak in her hair for a while. But apparently some didn't feel it was office-appropriate, so she saved it for shopping days. Now she dressed in wool suits, A-line skirts, and scratchy woven dresses to work. She painted on weekends and often went to galleries. When she threw a cocktail party, and she loved to entertain, someone invariably asked if any of her work on the walls was for sale. She blushed to cover her immense delight and said she didn't really think they were good enough. She did, though.

She was beginning to love working with Kevin. It was inspirational. He was young and very talented. A bit moody, but what artist isn't? They began to paint on weekends together when they both had time, exploring new artists and techniques. It was great having someone to talk with about art. Someone to work with. She didn't think Kevin really knew how good he actually was, but given time, his work would be in galleries. Of that she was sure. She often fantasized about opening a gallery of her own, stepping away from law, the suits and ties and narrow viewpoints about the world. But it paid the bills, and that was important.

A siren and flashing red lights screamed past the bus. Someone must be a having a baby, she thought. Better than contemplating a car wreck, internal bleeding, or brain damage. She noticed that there weren't too many people on the bus, a little less than half full. The lady sitting at the front was wearing an absolutely hideous fake fur coat, and her hair looked like a Crisco commercial. Thank God leopards didn't really look like that. The furniture in her home was probably that gross yellow vinyl stuff. Jina's apartment was tastefully decorated and sparse. One of her favourite pieces was the cream-coloured L-shaped couch that Lucy had chosen, covered with gently woven linen fabric. It was particularly comfortable when Lucy was lying on top of her. They never quite made it to the bedroom; it was up four stairs, after all. She should have called her to come and pick her up instead of taking the bus so late. They would have gone out for dinner. She couldn't remember why she hadn't done that.

A couple of kids sitting across from her had earbuds in place, but Jina could hear the pounding music. A sonata would have suited much better right now. She was feeling uneasy. She needed sugar or alcohol. She turned her head a little to the right to loosen some hair that got stuck on the frosted window and noticed a man sitting at the back of the bus. Not an unattractive man, around her age but a little careless — hair tousled, shirt collar half inside his tan jacket, half out, his face almost clean-shaven. But Jina was fixated by his brown eyes. She knew they were brown because they were staring right at her, through her.

Slightly distressed, she turned around and started to fiddle with the clasp on her briefcase. Why was he staring at her like that? Well, he certainly wouldn't waste his time staring at the lady in the fake leopard coat. Jina's stomach gave a quiet but insistent grumble. The flavour from her gum was making her hungrier now. She took it out of her mouth and began to roll it between her thumb and index finger. She tried to distract herself. Dinner. She'd probably have a salad for dinner, a little oil and vinegar dressing and then order a veggie pizza. There was probably a little wine left in the fridge, or some beer. Just thinking about it made her hungrier. Jina was always counting calories, whether she needed to or not. She never needed to. If the exercise program didn't keep her thin, her nervous energy did. She decided to text Lucy and let her know how hungry she was.

The bus came to a stop. The leopard coat got off, and an old man and two young girls got on. The bus started to move as the people staggered to their seats. The guy from the back had moved closer. He was almost right across from Jina now, still staring.

Jina was feeling more than slightly distressed now. A lump was forming in her chest, like someone had their fist there and was pushing. She turned and looked out the window. The dark night outside and the bright lights inside made the window into a mirror. She could see the man, still staring. It was even creepier seeing him stare from the slightly distorted glass reflection. She decided to look straight ahead, but her peripheral vision still caught his gaze. The fist was pushing harder now. The gum between her fingers was making her nervous. It was not too sticky any more, just hard and cold, so she pushed it under the seat. Normally she would wrap it in a small piece of paper and wait until she came to a trashcan. But she was anxious and didn't want the gum on her coat.

It wasn't too far now to Jina's stop on Primrose Street. She really did like the street. Not only were the maple trees just beautiful, but she had met some great people. Mary was a blast, and her friend Maggie, well, it was a shock when she found out that she and Tabitha were sisters.

A couple of men on the street were pretty rude. She tried to ignore the rude comments. Lucy always told her it would never change. *Just come home for a hug*, she would say. She was really looking forward to that hug now. She was also hoping that this guy would get off before she did. The bus stopped, but he didn't get off. Jina's heart beat a little faster. Next stop was hers. Maybe she should go and tell the driver that this guy was bothering her, but what would he say? A stare wasn't against the law. *Shit.*

Jina put on her gloves, picked up her briefcase, and stepped off the bus into the cold, black air. She started walking, trying not to look to see if he had left the bus. She did. He had. He was following. Her mind was racing in crazy directions. The fist was almost through to her spine now, and she could sense beads of sweat developing on her brow and between her breasts, despite the cold. This was the last time she would walk home alone or take that goddamn bus. Her boss could just fucking drive her home if he wanted her to work late. Right to her front door. Those strong thoughts made her settle a bit until she heard footsteps behind her, getting quicker and closer. She started walking a little faster, resisting the urge to run. Then his hand was on her shoulder. She froze. Her left arm clutched her briefcase, her right arm held the front of her coat together tightly. She couldn't feel her heartbeat — she could hear it.

"Hi, you're Jina Simpson, right? I wasn't sure, because you had your hair up when I came to your last party. You don't remember me, do you? I'm a friend of a guy at your office, he invited me to your…"

Jina wasn't afraid anymore — she was pissed off and had adrenaline stinging through her like angry hornets. She couldn't believe how casually he was just chatting after scaring the shit out of her. Her breath came in gasps, and he didn't even seem to notice.

"What the fuck…." she blurted out.

"Oh Jesus, I scared you. I'm so sorry, I didn't mean to scare you. Fuck. Listen, can I walk you home?"

Lucy would die when she heard this story. She would just pee her pants laughing.

"No, no, I'm good. But next time say hello on the bus."

Jina briskly walked home, leaving him standing alone on the sidewalk.

Cheryl can sit for hours, just staring at the bark of the maple tree in her backyard. And the tree will watch her, sap running along the outside edges of its wrinkled, hard bark, with no way to wipe it off. The bark will blur into shapes in front of her unblinking eyes, and she will see Derek smiling at her or busy with his crayons or paints. Sometimes it will be dusk before she pulls herself away, and only because it has become too dark to see clear lines as shadows begin to play on the tree.

Cheryl has trouble forgiving herself for waiting so long to end things with Robert. If she had stood up to him, made him leave earlier, Derek might still be alive. Sometimes she wonders if she'll ever sleep again. Days fold into other days that fold into other days.

No one really knows what happened in their house on Primrose Street, but there are rumours, many, many rumours. None as formidable as the real story. But when people aren't fed the truth, they need to nourish their curiosity, fill the gap and the lack of words with their own creations, add to the sticky web. It is hardest for Amanda, really. She was closer to Derek than anyone. She hears the whispers in town. She loved her brother and kept his secret close, to her heart, even as young girl. She had always known. When they were young and small, she would crawl into his bed late at night when she couldn't sleep, or vice versa, and they would lie together and talk. She knew how creative he was, how he felt trapped in his body. But she had no idea how to help him, who to tell. And she knew how her dad hated him. Hated him for everything he wasn't. Hated him for everything he was. It was Amanda who sat by his bed in the hospital when his father had first caught him in a dress and almost killed him. They continued to text and connect through social media when Derek left for school. She chose to go to med school in province, while Derek had left and gone out east. He said he wanted to get as far away as possible. If they'd had universities in the Arctic, he would have gone there.

He had called Amanda from school one day. He needed to talk. She could hear it in his voice. But she had had an exam that evening and had said they would talk soon. She was so glad he'd come home for Thanksgiving, but they didn't get a chance to be alone together. She had trouble forgiving herself for not making time for him that day he called. She should have blown off the exam. She often wondered if she could have saved him, helped him find a different solution from the one he was obviously contemplating. He had wanted to talk when he called; she should have recognized that. Maybe it would have made a difference. She promised she would never be too busy again if someone needed to talk. Her scar was deep. Deep and painful and weeping.

Cheryl had just closed the door to Derek's room that fateful day. The grey wall beside the bed was splattered with red. It looked like someone had squirted a cherry Slurpee all over the wall. Small beads of red extended to smaller dots and faded to nothing, extending down the wall behind the bed. Graham came in and washed the wall, rearranged the room, opened the window, and took the comforter away. She's turned Derek's room into a solarium. The new glass wall and door brings lots of light into the house, and she fills the room with plants.

Cheryl wants to leave Primrose Street. No one can blame her. But a geographical fix never really fixes anything. She would miss her daughter, her friends. So a luncheon is planned between Cheryl, Jina, Maggie, and Mary. A subtle intervention of sorts. Christine can't make it and neither can Ruth, and Cora isn't feeling well. But the other four have decided to start the luncheon tradition. It is time for a little fun.

They choose a small little café in town, one that uses Graham's bread for their sandwiches.

A reservation card sits on a round table at the back. It is a quaint bistro, maybe ten tables in total. A light blue tablecloth hangs over the edges of each table, one tall daisy in a thin glass vase sits in the centre. They all arrive at different times and collect at the round table near the back.

"I'm so glad we all did this. Thank you," begins Jina.

"Yes, I can't remember the last time we all got together, other than a street meeting," says Cheryl.

"Well, we thought it was time. And it is a good opportunity to welcome Jina to the street and see if we can get you to stay, Cheryl," says Maggie. Both women smile.

"I mean, we chat across the sidewalk, but now it's a bit easier to hear what you're saying. You know? So, tell us how you are liking Martineville, Jina," says Mary.

"It's a nice town. It seems to have everything you need, not too small, not too big, just right." There is a chuckle around the table. The waitress comes over to their table.

"Ready to order?"

"Right, sorry," they seem to say in unison as they bury themselves in the menu.

Maggie makes a suggestion. "The quiche and a salad look good." She glances over the top of her menu.

"Sounds good, I'll have the same," says Mary.

"Make that three."

"And four."

"To drink?" asks the server.

The ladies glance at each other coyly. "A glass of red wine?" suggests Cheryl.

"May I suggest a carafe?" offers the server.

"You certainly may," says Maggie. "In fact, let's have two carafes."

"Oh, I don't know, Maggie..."

"Cheryl, enjoy." Cheryl refolds her napkin and smiles.

"Okay, I'll be right back with your wine." The ladies settle back into conversation.

"Where did you live before?" Maggie asks Jina.

"A small town just east of Toronto."

"So what brought you here?"

"The job. I wanted to work at a law firm that was a bit smaller before I tried for Toronto. That's where I'd like to end up."

"Why Toronto?"

"I did my degree there, and I really liked it. But my partner liked the idea of a smaller town, so we're trying this on for size." The waitress arrives, places three red wine glasses with long stems on the table, and begins to pour small amounts of the bold red liquid into each one. She leaves the carafe on the table and quietly leaves. They each pick up a glass, look at each other, and lift their glasses.

"Cheers," says Maggie.

"To new friendships," says Mary.

"New friendships," they all say together and clink glasses, but before they can take a sip Cheryl adds, "and wonderful old ones."

"To friends," they all chant together. They take a sip, savouring the flavour.

"Well, Martineville has a lot to offer," Maggie continues talking to Jina, "but Primrose Street is like a town on its own."

"Yes, I have noticed that. It's pretty unique."

"Yeah, Primrose Street has a dynamic all its own, that's for sure," offers Mary.

"That was clear at the last street meeting," says Jina. "Seemed a bit over the top just for one piece of sidewalk."

"Some residents on the street do like things over the top," Maggie says. "I grew up with the biggest one. But you know, I think sometimes they have these little meetings just as a reason to get everyone together."

"Not sure I'll attend another one," says Jina.

"Why's that, Jina?" asks Mary.

"Well, there were some pretty rude comments that I overheard," says Cheryl. "My past husband was part of that. I'm sorry, Jina."

"Yes, I heard that too. My dad was part of it too. It is embarrassing. I apologize for my father, again and again and again. Please don't judge the town or street just based on Don."

"Or based on Robert."

"Oh God, when those two get together, it isn't pretty."

"Oh God, yes, I try to forget," said Cheryl. "I am so very sorry. Well, at least we won't have to worry about that happening anymore. Robert and Don getting together."

"Really, it's okay," said Jina. "That's one of the reasons I want to move to Toronto. It isn't perfect, but with more people, there's a greater chance of fitting in, or at least getting lost in the crowd. I've just had enough of those comments."

"Well, we hope you don't leave too fast. Maybe you'll change your mind," says Mary.

"Thanks."

"Anything we can say to change your mind, Cheryl?" asks Mary. "We know Amanda doesn't want to see you go, and neither do we. Where will you go?"

"I don't know. Maybe the west coast? Or maybe France."

"Why not just travel for a while, get some space, and then come back. Moving, selling, it's such a big deal. You've been through a lot. Careful not to do too much right now, you know, really big changes," says Mary.

"I never thought of just travelling. I could go for a number of months."

"And you could go to a number of countries. Just really see the world," says Jina. "I'd love to be able to do that."

"I would miss being here. And I would miss Amanda and Sam."

"So moving isn't the answer. Why not just do some small trips? Maybe you can get my mother to go with you. God knows she needs to get out, get some perspective," says Maggie.

"You make a good point. I could travel first and think of moving after. But I'll need some help with arrangements. I've never done anything like this before. I always dreamed I'd marry someone who would do those things with me. I just don't know how it all went so wrong. Robert always had an edge, but he wasn't cruel. Or at least I didn't want to see it."

"It's so hard to know," says Mary.

"And then Derek." It is the perfect moment for the food to arrive, and they all take advantage of the moment to gather their cutlery, place their napkins, and ooo and aaa over the quiche and salad.

"Hmmm, wonderful dressing on the salad," says Jina. "Lucy would love this. We'll have to come here sometime."

"Great quiche. I never would have thought of this kind of cheese and vegetable together," says Mary.

"Well, you are the cheese girl," offers Maggie, and everyone smiles, chewing happily, a tense moment bypassed.

"Yeah, I guess I just got lucky with Daniel," says Maggie. "Not really sure how that happened. I never even really dated in high school. But I always had a crush on this one guy. Didn't think he even knew I existed. Funny how wrong we can be about people."

"What do you mean?" asks Jina.

"Well, he apparently watched me all through high school but didn't think I'd say yes. Thought I was too involved in school stuff. And all I was thinking was God, I wish he'd ask me out. Funny. And now, Daniel and I have a really honest, fantastic relationship. We got together right at the end of high school, stayed in touch through university, and just couldn't imagine not being together. Kind of a fairy tale, I guess." Everyone takes a mouthful and Maggie continues. "When we first hooked up, he drove me home after the last high school party, and his kiss lingered on my lips for days. Then we had our first date later that week, and we ended up having this incredible sex in the back of his car when he drove me home. Don't tell Mom, Cheryl." Maggie gives Cheryl a wide-eyed stare and laughs. "But it wasn't like turn off the lights, hide under the covers, don't say a word, get in, get out. You know. It was passion, long, lingering, hot passion. We talked. He asked. I answered. And it hasn't changed. We tell each other our fantasies, sometimes read erotic stories together."

Mouths stop chewing for a moment as eyes widen around the table. "No, seriously, everyone thinks about it, everyone wants to explore, but it's this big secret. So we decided no secrets. And it's kind of weird how everyone wants something exciting, but with someone else. So we get the exciting together, which is really exciting. And everything else seems to be different because of that. We just communicate together, good and not so good." Maggie sits back and sips her wine, Daniel popping into her mind.

"Wow. That's wonderful, Mag. Really. You've had a hard time with your dad and sister. You deserve this," says Mary.

"What about Graham, Mary, come on," goads Maggie. "Your turn."

Mary blushes, takes a sip of her wine, and leans back in her chair. "Graham is so tender and gentle, and making love is so beautiful, but I don't know if I could tell him my fantasies. I think some things are better left in the imagination, unspoken."

"I used to think that too, but being open means everything is open. You and Graham are so great together, seriously, Mary, I bet he'd love it," says Maggie. "Come on, what are you afraid of?"

"Geez, I don't know, Mag. That would be a big change. I don't know if I could do that."

"Come on, Mary, don't you think about Graham in naughty ways? He's so handsome."

"I think like that about Lucy," says Jina. "She's beautiful. And now that you've said it like that, I see your point. Makes me think. I'd like to know her fantasies, maybe she'd like to know mine."

"Exactly. Give it a shot." There is a moment of silence as they chew and savour the wine and the friendship.

"Quiche is good," says Mary.

"Yes, this is a great place for lunch," says Cheryl.

"Let's make it more often together," suggests Mary.

"Okay, how about this," says Maggie. "You're not getting off that easy. You girls think about saying something bold to your lovers, and next lunch we'll compare stories."

There is nervous, excited laughter.

"I'll think about it," says Mary.

"No way, you do more than think about it, girlfriend," pokes Maggie.

"I'm in," says Jina. "What about Cheryl?"

"Oh, I'm too old for that. Plus, I'm alone now. Not that it would ever have been an option before. I can't ever remember even liking sex. I'm feeling jealous. I hope my girl has what you girls have. Maggie, you should talk to her."

"Actually, you should talk to her, Cheryl. So that's your piece. You tell us what happens when you talk to Amanda. Just tell her about our lunch and see what she says. I bet you'll be surprised. And it will open up your relationship together. Might even help her."

"I don't know."

"Come on, Cheryl," says Mary. "It's time for a change. I think Maggie's idea is a good one."

"Jina?"

"Yup, me too."

Cheryl is a select shade of pink and starts sipping her wine. "Fine," is all she can manage. They are all smiling, including Cheryl. It feels good to smile.

"Okay. So now, Jina, tell me, honestly, what is it like to work with my little sister?" asks Maggie.

"Now we are getting into fantasies," says Jina. They all laugh and refill their wine glasses. "No talk of your sister."

"It would certainly be a different kind of lunch if she was invited," adds Cheryl.

"Yes, for sure," says Jina. "But you know who we should have invited?"

"Who?" they all say simultaneously.

"Amiritha."

"Oh yeah, you're right," say Maggie. "She's really lovely. I've seen such a difference in Justin lately."

"It's true," says Cheryl. "And Kevin too, although he'd never admit it."

"So true," says Maggie. "Okay, I am putting a note in my phone right now to ask her to our next luncheon."

"Anything else I can get for you ladies? Coffee, desserts?"

"Well, I'm thinking another carafe of wine," says Maggie. "Girls?"

"Yes, we're not ready for coffee yet," says Jina, and they all laugh together.

"Another carafe coming up," says the waitress, clearly enjoying her table.

FOURTEEN PRIMROSE STREET: KEVIN

"I don't know, Justin, it's…"

"Amiritha, please, just go and see what the situation is. I just can't leave work until I finish analyzing this one slide in the lab. Probably late, and that could be too late. Know what I mean? Please."

"He doesn't like me, Justin. He won't like me being there without you."

"Oh Ami, that's not true."

"It is, he's never even said my name out loud. You just want it to be different."

"Maybe, I don't know, but please just go over and see if the cat is really dead. I wouldn't want him to bury her alive. Come on, you know you'd like an excuse to get out of the apartment. And it will give you a fresh look at your work when you get back. Please?"

"It's all very weird, but okay, for you. And you're right, I could use a break. I'm a little stuck. But if there is a problem, will you at least keep your phone right beside you? I don't want to be dead too."

"He's not that bad, Ami. He is just a kid."

"He's a big boy, Justin, and has a bad temper."

"You just haven't seen the other side. It's just, well, listen they're calling me. Please, Ami, please just check."

"Fine, I'll go."

"Call me, okay?"

"Okay."

She put down her iPhone and looked out the window. It was dull and grey, but she had come to accept that the sun hid more in North America than in Asia. She wondered if there would be any sun shining at Justin's house today. She just dreaded going over there alone. His son, Kevin, was surly to say the least. His other son had already left home and rarely returned to visit. Justin's divorce had been ugly. But after a year, Kevin had made it clear it was his house and Amiritha wasn't welcome.

She looked out the window to see what coat she should take. She couldn't get used to trees with no leaves. And she couldn't get used to so many different wardrobes for so much different weather. The daffodils in her neighbour's yard were poised to unfurl into spring, and the trees would soon follow with their greenery, but it was never soon enough for her. She loved the swaying, laughing daffodil petals. They really were a celebration to the end of winter. Seasons were new to her, and she loved them. They meant life had rhythm and colour and shape and change. Where she had grown up, it was like one season, one temperature, one set of clothes and footwear. Seasons. It was one of the many things she was coming to love about this place, this country. And then there was Justin. He was like no man she had ever met, with his unabashed shows of affection and how he really listened to her, a woman. New and radiant territory to be sure.

She went in search of her running shoes and her coat. It was still chilly outside. Crocuses and daffodils were famous for sporting a little leftover winter frost or snow, but she would need her winter coat. She loved how warm and soft it was; she had been tempted to wear it to bed in the really cold months. It was one of the first things she had bought after arriving from across the ocean.

As Amiritha turned the key in the lock of her small basement apartment door and stepped outside the house onto Richmond Street, she felt the winter spring breeze around her shoulders and pulled her coat closer to her face. The one thing she had loved about those cold winter days were evenings with Justin by his fireplace. He would snuggle her tiny frame against him on the couch, and they would watch silly movies together and laugh. She loved how he smelled of wood and work and maple syrup with pancakes. Now there was a food she had come to love; it was so different from the flavours she was accustomed to.

Her first year had been hard with no friends, and being the oldest in her class at the university didn't make that any easier. Winter had been a shock. She hadn't felt her toes for at least four months. This past winter had been warmer and more bearable because of Justin. She would have left months ago if it hadn't been for him. She smiled to herself. Who would have thought slipping on an iced-over puddle could change your life? When everyone else just stared at her, clutching at her ankle and crying in pain, Justin had walked right over, offered his arm, and taken her to the hospital emergency room. He smiled warmly as she struggled with her English and her tears, helping as much as he could. Pain and fear made it difficult to remember the new and foreign language. She was glad she wasn't alone. They wrapped her sprained ankle and gave her crutches, which turned out to be highly dangerous on the ice, but Justin steadied her as they left the hospital and took her for a coffee. They had met often since that day, Justin using the excuse that he wanted to make sure she was getting along okay with those crutches.

She walked along the sidewalk and was still surprised that she drew attention. She never could tell exactly why. Her skin colour? Her walk? Her manner? They couldn't smell food she prepared walking down the street, or how she worshipped. Sometimes it didn't feel like she had immigrated from another country — it felt like she'd travelled to another planet. People looked similar — they had two eyes, a nose, a mouth, ears on either side of the head, two arms and legs — but that was where any similarity ended, it seemed. Nothing was familiar outside of that. People talked about their feelings, they looked you straight in the eye, they talked behind your back, they were afraid of skin colour. Trains were on schedule, banks took less than two hours to meet your needs, food was easy to get and plentiful, and there was such variety, houses were big, sewers were hidden, water was clean, women had rights. And now here she was being asked to go and see if a cat was really dead because a teenage boy was not willing or able, hard to know. Justin didn't want the cat buried alive. It was all incomprehensible to her, but she had great respect and admiration for Justin, and this must be really important in ways she couldn't understand, or he wouldn't have asked. She felt a warm glow all over her body these days when she heard his voice or pictured him in her mind.

She daydreamed as she walked. She wondered if her mother was making her favourite foods that day. She so missed shahi tuukra, a dessert so delicious. And her mother could make the best naan. She could buy that in the big city, but not in Martineville. She had been able to make some good daal because lentils were easy to get, and stew was good in these cold temperatures. Justin loved her daal. And he liked it when she made biryani with different meat each time.

"You're such a fantastic cook," he would say.

"Only because my mother isn't here. To taste her food is to taste food. If you ever come to Pakistan, I will ask her to make a chicken karahi. That is good cooking."

"Well, in the meantime, I will keep enjoying yours. And maybe we'll drive into the city once in a while to pick up some naan for you and other spices you need." And that was one of the many reasons she was falling in love with him, and why she was walking over to check on a boy and a maybe dead cat.

She missed her mother. And her brother. But she had been accepted to study engineering at the local university on a scholarship, and she would never have had that chance in her home country. She was past the marrying age, past the anything age, and apparently no one wanted her now at the ripe age of twenty-nine. She had become a disgrace to her family. Her mother said otherwise, but she knew how deep her culture ran. No matter — she didn't want what they had to offer anyway. Coming abroad opened her world, and she had met Justin. But she was homesick. Sometimes she didn't really know why. There was less fear here, no lack of food or entertainment, more opportunities. And yet the land didn't speak to her. She was lost in a world with different-coloured soil, different-coloured people, white blankets outside in winter, evergreen trees, tiny occasional flowers, and a temperature that always left her cold.

She rounded the corner of Richmond Street and turned onto Primrose Street, making her way to the front door of Justin's house. She walked down the sidewalk and waved at Cora Burke.

Gently, she knocked on the door. No answer. She tried a few more times. No answer. She was reluctant to continue, but she had said yes, so she opened the unlocked door, which meant Kevin was home. She stood on the threshold and listened.

She heard some shuffling upstairs and a muted voice. She went up the stairs like a feline hoping to avoid its predator.

"Kevin?" Nothing. "Kevin?"

"In here," came a quiet, flat voice. Not the Kevin she was familiar with. She followed the voice down a cream-coloured hall with some small, framed drawings pencilled by children hanging on the wall. She stopped in the doorway and peered around the frame. There, sitting on the edge of the double bed, was the large frame of a rather lost youth hunched over a furry grey bundle in his lap, his long, brown, curly, unkempt hair falling onto the side of his pale, tear-streaked face. She moved over and sat down beside him, not saying a word and barely making an impression on the blue comforter. She folded her hands in her lap and waited as she had been instructed to do time and time again as she was growing up. Waiting was what women in her culture did best. Waiting to speak, sometimes for hours. Waiting to eat until Father took the first bite, or husband, which might be after he finished reading that page of the newspaper. Waiting for the bus, not knowing if it would even come that day. Waiting for her mother to lift her eyes after a man had left the room. And so she waited.

They sat like that for a long time. Finally, she reached up and put her hand tenderly on his shoulder. He was shaking ever so slightly, as a leaf on a maple tree in autumn almost ready to fall to the ground.

"She was a good cat, you know." He pulled his nose. "She used to sit on the back of the chair in the living room and lick my neck, like I was one of her kittens and she had to clean me. Mom thought it was disgusting when she did that. But Bubbles was looking after me."

Silence again.

"I'd see her waiting in the window for me as I walked home from school, and then when I came in, she would be at the door, waiting beside my mother. When Mom was passed out on the couch, it would be Bubbles alone waiting at the door."

Amiritha put her hand back into her lap.

"I'll miss her," he barely whispered. Silence. Waiting.

"She knows," Amiritha carefully offered. He turned and looked at her, maybe for the first time.

"How do you know?" But he wasn't being rude or condescending — he was searching. He wanted to know about this little friend he was cradling in his large arms.

"Because all creatures have a soul, and they never forget a kindness."

"Does she know I loved her?"

"Yes, she does."

"How can I make sure she remembers me?"

He pulled the cat closer. Back home, a man of his age would probably already have a wife, children, a job, and years of experience, not always pleasant. Here at the same age most people had more education, studied at universities, and were well on their way to a career, but they didn't have a sense of self or family or community. And here she was, sitting beside this boy/man who was asking the questions of a child. Amiritha reached over to check the pulse on the cat's neck. Very lifeless and getting colder quickly. Dead for sure.

"Well, maybe you could think of something special that we could put into her grave with her."

"Like what?"

"Something to take with her into the next world for comfort and memories."

"What could it be? What could I give her" He was like a small child trying to make meaning out of a painful loss. Something he had not been able to do with his past.

"What do you have that we could wrap into the towel she's lying in?"

Silence. Waiting. Kevin stood, cradling the cat, which was getting stiffer with every minute, into the crook of his arm, and left the room.

She waited. He returned with a small pair of scissors and stood facing her.

"I don't really have anything small enough, but how about cutting off a small piece of my hair? She liked to chew it when we'd play on the floor. Would that work?"

He had accepted her offering so easily, and she felt touched and honoured. She was cautious and slow with her words.

"Yes, that would be perfect. I think that would be very special to her."

He handed her the scissors, and she stood up on her tiptoes to cut a piece off his hair at the back. She took the lock and laid it carefully beside the cat nestled in the towel.

"Kevin, we can't bury her today, the ground is still too frozen. But we don't want her to, well, get worse. What do you think?"

"Can we put her in the freezer until the earth softens? Can you come back to help bury her then?"

She smiled. "Yes, I'll come back. The freezer is a good idea until then."

"Can you come downstairs with me?"

"I can."

Bubbles, the dead cat, a bridge between cultures. The missing ingredient that made her feel like maybe, just maybe, Martineville could be her home. So off they went, down the cream-coloured hall, past the pencil drawings, down the stairs, through the kitchen, down more stairs, into the basement, and into the room with the freezer. They stood before it as it if were a coffin lined with gold. Kevin opened the lid and carefully laid his precious bundle wrapped in the towel with his tresses into one of the freezer's food baskets near the top. The lid closed, and years of tears filled his yes. Amiritha reached up and put her arm on his.

"Shall we say a prayer for her?" she offered with more confidence. He nodded, not trusting himself to speak.

"We hope that Bubbles will be cared for in the next world as she was cared for here and that she will know how much she was loved. Amen."

He started to cry. And soon his big body was draped around her tiny figure, sobbing and shaking. She was a little worried that she would not be able to support him, but he clung to her tightly. And she waited.

They stayed like that a long time, until finally he straightened and began wiping his eyes and nose on his sleeve. He was hunched over and looking down. Something needed to be said, so she reached out to her mother for help and remembered her rich and warm hugs and words that would hang like honey around her when she was scared or lonely. She spoke softly.

"Thank you, Kevin, for sharing this with me and trusting me." A tear slipped down her dark-skinned cheek.

He straightened out of his hunch and looked directly at her.

"No, thank..." and the moment suspended itself like a hovering dove, "thank you... Amiritha."

The maples on the street hang like weeping willows as Jina calls 911. She hears the screams from across the road. Peter hears them too, like a wounded animal. Amanda is visiting her mother and hears the wails while they are having coffee together. Even Cora down the road hears the painful lament as she prunes her roses. The sound catches in the maple's leaves, sending shivers and quivers through the branches. The trees tremble as if caught in a gale.

Amanda arrives first. Mary is standing paralyzed in the front yard, Graham at her feet, barely breathing. Amanda rushes to where Graham is lying on the ground. She rips open his shirt and begins pounding his chest and then gives him mouth-to-mouth. Her CPR is rigorous. Amanda is focused on keeping him breathing until the paramedics arrive. She doesn't notice others arriving.

Jina walks quickly across the street, calling Maggie on her cellphone as she approaches Mary, who stands frozen. Pale. Rigid. Terrified. Jina comes and put her arms around her shoulders. They are shaking in rhythm with her body.

"Is he still breathing, is he, is he still breathing?" she imperceptibly whispers to Jina.

"Yes, he's still breathing. Amanda is keeping him breathing."

"He's still breathing, okay, okay." Peter arrives and goes over to Mary. She reaches for his arm, fingers digging into his skin.

"Is he still breathing, Peter, is he, is he?"

"Yes, Mary, I'm sure he is." But he isn't sure, he isn't sure at all. Graham is lying in a very contorted position on the ground. Mrs. Burke goes over, rolls up her jacket, and tucks it under his head. There is a big bump on the side of his head. He must have hit the rock in the garden as he fell. His usually sunny face is shadowed, white, and his lips are turning blue.

It is clear to everyone how much Mary and Graham have cared for each other. They would be seen reaching for each other's hands in public and always standing very close. Graham would watch Mary with longing, and she would always smile when she caught his eye. They had a new bench in their garden, right under the biggest maple with the most shade. They would often sit there together, his arm draped over her shoulders, intently listening as she spoke. The maple would circle gentle breezes around them that followed them into their bedroom on warm evenings. Graham would pull her close to him as he crawled into bed, place his lips on hers, and linger there as she moved into him. Their lovemaking was passionate and gentle all at the same time. Their skin glistened with intention and desire as their limbs bent and moved with increasing rhythm. They craved each other with tongues and whispered words of longing and gratitude. His fingers would stroke her neck as she came, and she would tuck her face against his cheek as he released into her while wrapping his arm around her waist and the other under her left thigh. After, she would move her back against his chest, he would tuck his one arm under her neck and the other over her body, cradling her breast in his hand. Her hand would move on top of his and their fingers interlaced. He would kiss her ear, tell her he loved her, and they would drift into sleep, breezes dancing through the room.

It hadn't always been like that for Graham. Although everyone thought he had been crushed by his first wife's illness and subsequent death, he had in fact been relieved. It was a rare occasion when he would come home and not be nagged or yelled at for one thing or another. It was as if she resented his gentle nature, wanted to provoke him to wrath, and yet he never bit, which enraged her even more. Knowing he was allergic to garlic, she prepared an elaborate meal one weekend, a baked whole chicken with over fourteen cloves of garlic as stuffing. She didn't tell Graham, and he was violently sick afterward. He never said a thing. He would renovate the bathroom, and she would berate him for the tiles on the floor, even though they were her choice. She told him he was gangly and that his penis was too small and she couldn't have sex because of how he smelled. And when she died he didn't keep the garden up for her; he could finally plant things he wanted and not be chastised.

Mary had given him life. She complimented things he did, said how handsome he was, how good he smelled. At first he thought she was teasing him, but after time passed and she continued to say the same things, he realized she was sincere. Slowly, he realized how cruel his deceased wife had been.

He had stopped wanting to have sex with her, but with Mary desires returned, and she was agreeable and grateful for his touch, his kisses, his body. He started to laugh more, enjoy doing work around the house, and joyfully anticipated going to bed each night. Customers noticed the difference as well.

"How's it going, Graham?" they would ask.

"My life is fucking fantastic," he would say, beaming from ear to ear.

Mary felt the same. She became a sunny, energetic woman who talked quickly and a lot. But she was passionate and kind. Not everyone saw that in Mary, especially her ex. One evening, when she was trying to explain to him why she wanted different furniture in the living room, he had yelled at her, "Shut up, you bitch, stop your incessant talking." He hit her so hard across the head that he damaged the hearing in her left ear. She always thought it was her fault. If she just didn't talk so much, or want things done differently, everything would be fine. It was never going to be fine, and she soon realized that. Eventually, she walked out, taking nothing.

Maggie had been there for Mary when she left her first husband. She stayed with Maggie and Daniel for almost six months until she was able to find a job and a place to live. Then she and Maggie began their weekly outings. She loved those outings. And of course, one of those excursions changed her life. Graham, slowly, with his gentle strength, his patience, his love, helped Mary begin to find her self-esteem again. She started to laugh out loud without worrying. She would talk about things she loved, add her opinion to conversations and not feel invisible. One evening, they were discussing changes they wanted to make to the kitchen and Mary stopped talking and began to cry.

"What, what is it Mary?"

"I'm sorry, I'm sorry I want to change things," she cried.

"Why do you say that? It's a good idea, I love your ideas."

"You do? Really?"

"Of course, I do. I love how you talk a mile a minute when you get excited. I love how you see everything coming together and the colours you pick; I could never see things the way you do. I love your big, bold laugh." He walked over and wiped the tears from her face and pulled her close to him. "I love YOU."

She had clung to him. They clung to each other.

There is a cluster of neighbours around Graham now. Some are standing beside Mary, but she keeps walking away, coming back, walking away, coming back. Maggie arrives as quickly as she can and runs over to her friend. She pulls her into her arms and holds her close. Mary is a stick figure. No movement, no tears, no life.

"Mary, you're shivering. Let's get you a jacket."

"Is he breathing Maggie, is he, is he breathing?" Her voice is like a wizened piece of fruit on a counter.

"I don't know, honey, I don't know." Mary buries her head into Maggie's shoulder, suspended, as if hanging from a thin rope deep down in a dark, cold, mouldering well, and at any moment the rope could snap and there will be no way out.

The paramedics arrive and shock him into life, his chest lurching up in the garden, under the arch where he married his love. People stand back as they strap Graham to a board and carry him into the ambulance. Amanda hops in with him and waves to Mary. She doesn't attempt a smile. The doors to the ambulance close.

"Was he breathing, Maggie, was he?"

TWENTY-FIVE PRIMROSE STREET: MARY

Mary stood at the opening of her closet. She glanced among the summer dresses that hung on limp hangers, a few special occasion dresses, her blouses and slacks, and then her eyes glazed over as the hangers curled inside Graham's extra-large sweaters, collar shirts with matching ties wrapped around the hangers, a few pairs of dress slacks, and then t-shirts and jeans. She reached out and stroked the sleeve of the brown woven sweater, bringing the cuff to her face, inhaling the fragrant aroma that was uniquely his, then pulling her hand through the collared shirts and pausing on the jeans. He looked so good in a pair of jeans.

Tears that had welled up in her eyes spilled over, disappearing into her skin. She put her hand between his clothes and hers and gently pushed his collection to one side. She considered her options for the day and pulled out a dark blue blouse and some black slacks. Her world had turned black and white, and she had no desire to wear any other hue. She didn't feel inclined to adorn herself with earrings or makeup. She made herself pull a brush through her hair, noticing the dark circles under her eyes matched her outfit. She put on her silver Elle watch with the ruby on the second hand. He had given it to her on their first Christmas together. It was beautiful, and he was thrilled at how she loved it immediately. She clasped it onto her wrist as she remembered the moment, how she couldn't believe how much he had spent on her, how perfectly he knew her taste. She pulled on a creamy white cotton sweater with pearl buttons down the front. It was the last gift he had given her, just a happy Wednesday gift. He would do things like that, just surprise her one day. She had worn it every day since he died. Sometimes even to bed at night. She pulled it around and close to her body and went downstairs to the kitchen, as if sleepwalking.

It was her first day back at work since Graham had died. She had been given five days off. Five days to deal with the funeral home, insurance companies, neighbours, and try to look at herself in the mirror. Five days was what they deemed his life had been worth to her. Nine if you count the weekends, front and back. There was no need to pack a lunch. She ate very little these days, finding it hard to swallow and harder to digest. She made a tea with some honey and put it in a travel mug for the drive. She had been feeling dizzy as of late and had already lost over ten pounds. She had been advised at least to drink something nourishing. Tea and honey was the best she could manage.

She was frustrated by her human condition. Her body hurt. Muscles deep beneath the surface screamed with rage at two in the morning. She took painkillers and curled around a heating pad, hoping for a bit more sleep. She craved numbing substances. Her neck refused to move easily. Turning her head was like a maple branch torn reluctantly off a tree, creating splinters of pain. There was no relief. There was nowhere to run.

She locked the door of the house as she walked out to the car, putting her purse on the passenger seat beside the Kleenex box. She had become brilliant at crying these days, and Kleenex were staples. Her hands rested on the steering wheel. She sat and stared at the road ahead. It felt as if she were embarking on a journey to Alaska rather than a mere thirty-minute drive down the road. And Graham wasn't there to see her off. Every morning he would help her carry things to the car or scrape off the ice and snow in the winter before she came outside. He'd kiss her, tell her to drive carefully, and wave as she pulled out. He never missed a morning. She put the car into gear and inched down the driveway like someone with a learner's permit. She passed under the low-hanging maple branches, and her eyes welled up again, making it hard to see. She stopped and pulled a Kleenex out of the box, dabbing her eyes.

It was under the maples that he had fallen. It was where she had felt his last breath on her cheek. His blue lips told her he was gone. No time to say goodbye. No time to say she loved him. She had stepped back as the paramedics stepped in. It was over, and she cared not to watch the futile and brutal attempt to start his heart again as he lay motionless. She crawled away, dazed, and curled around the daisies in the flower garden they had planted together. He choosing one plant, her another. He had always patiently waited with shovel in hand as she tiptoed to find the perfect spot for the next occupant. Their garden proudly bloomed from April to October. When a plant would come into bloom, he would wait for her excited response, and they would both go to admire the flower. She would call them by name, and he would admire their colours as he tucked her under his arm and kissed the side of her head. The daisies were her favourite. Graham always remembered and loved to bring her bouquets of daisies. After a long day at work, she would walk in the door to daisies smiling on the dining room table.

She had last seen him in a hospital emergency room, tubes protruding from his mouth, needles left in his arms, skin yellowing. It didn't smell like him anymore. It was truly only a shell that once housed her love, a man who believed in her, understood her. She tentatively leaned over the tubes and needles and kissed his cheek one last time, whispering that she loved him. Her whispers were absorbed by the clinical voice crowding the loudspeaker, footfalls of attendants in the halls and the wheels of the stretchers as they were pushed down an endlessly echoing hall. Nurses and attendants were moving other patients in and out of emergency rooms. She turned to leave, eyeing no one, purse dragging on the sanitized hospital floor, and passed through the exit.

She left pieces of herself in that emergency room. The rain began. Salty, endless storms of tears, making driving dangerous and functioning impossible. It rained and rained and rained. The thunder and lightning were terrifying, shaking the foundations of all her belief systems.

Now she sat, engine running, blankly watching a car drive by, and laboriously pulled out behind it, accelerating to the speed limit. It was the first time she had left the house in days, but it seemed like months, maybe years since she had been outside. It was her only connection with him now, their house, their home, and part of her was terrified that by leaving, that last thread would be severed. Just this morning she remembered seeing his reading glasses resting on his open book he had left on his bedside table. She had left his balled-up sock on the floor where he had dropped it and couldn't remember why it had ever caused her such irritation. Their wedding photo seemed ancient, people from another story. Her toothbrush sat beside his on the vanity, his razor in its holder. Shoes and boots tucked under the bench by the front door, waiting, his parka hollow on its hook. Ray-Ban sunglasses folded around his keys on the hall table. Graham was everywhere. He was nowhere. She felt her heart begin to race, and beads of perspiration collected on her forehead as more tears rolled out of her eyes. She reached for another Kleenex.

Sense memory led her to her parking spot at work. She had not touched her tea yet, so she took that with her, along with her purse. She stuffed handfuls of Kleenex into her pockets and attempted a deep breath, putting one foot in front of the other to reach the front door. It was a long walk, as if through a vacuum. She pulled open the front door and walked to her office. Thin smiles greeted her. She didn't know how to respond. A few colleagues ventured forward to speak.

"How are you?" they asked.

"Do you really want that answer?" she imperceptibly replied.

Nothing more was said, and she continued to the conference room for the meeting she had been emailed about. She felt as if she were inside a glass bubble. The lips of others around the table were moving. She could see them but couldn't hear a sound. She was isolated in her silence. Her grief was palatable.

Papers were circulated around the table. Her eyes focused on a random word here or there, but she found it difficult to concentrate on reading a whole sentence. Her mind went back to her home. She felt panicked at being so far away. Her heart was as thin and cracked as a maple leaf at the end of autumn, easily torn and crumpled. Fragile, tender. The space between living and falling into a deep dark hole was so slight, she dared not look out from under her eyelashes for fear the movement would push her over the edge. She dabbed at her eyes with a Kleenex and moved her pen across the page in front of her. She tried to swallow a sip of her tea and noticed a warmth slip down her throat. She took another sip.

Mary's day at work was a collection of cold silence, broken thoughts, and disconnected work sheets. She looked at the same screen on her laptop for thirty minutes before clicking another button. "She's doing so well," she heard people whisper, relieved that she didn't speak of her grief, grief that made them quiver in their own skin. People tired quickly of grief, but it didn't seem to tire of her. She felt like she was standing in a cyclone, yet everyone outside was moving so slowly. She wasn't aware it was time to leave until she saw others moving around with briefcases in hand and outside coats.

She was exhausted by the time she climbed back into the driver's seat. As she drove home, the car veered onto the shoulder a few times as her eyes closed. The noise of the gravel under the tires and the jolt of the car awakened her. Her fatigue was deeper than muscle tissue. She opened the window and turned up the radio in order to get home. After what seemed an eternity, she drove past the maples and into her driveway.

There were fleeting instances when she sensed he was near. She'd turn to see if someone was behind, the sense of being so strong. The alarm on her cellphone would randomly begin, but it was not the ring she had set. Tears escaped her eyes, burning the already salted red skin on her face. She wanted to close her eyes and reach out and feel him at the ends of her fingertips. She wanted to wake up from this endless, open-eyed nightmare.

She walked in through the front door and felt the emptiness. The silence was an assault. She never realized the mere energy of another person created sound in a house. She always knew how rich things were when he was there, but the intensity of his presence was only truly felt and understood with his absence. And not like someone away on a trip or at work, that still held sound and resonance. This was absolute. It was like everything was covered in white, white snow and not a breath of wind. She stood, lost, in its centre. Empty rooms screaming. His favourite chair stark as snow piled up around and inside it, no form to keep it warm and melt the coldness. She struggled not to be buried under the avalanche.

As days passed, she found herself caught in the routine of taking tea and honey as she robotically drove to work, only to face the cyclone inside the glass bubble. Driving always made Mary nervous. The car slipping if it hydroplaned would make her heart skip a beat. Other drivers not paying attention, veering into her lane, made her hold her breath. Like clockwork, Graham would call her at those moments. His calm and loving voice would help her relax and make better driving decisions. And then it hit her, taking her breath away: *There is no one who cares or will even notice if I arrive home.* With that realization, she began to sob, gasping for air, the road blurring in front of her. She had to pull over to recover herself before trusting herself with the wheel again.

Soon she became tired of feeding the darkness. She became sick of being the hunted.

One morning, sipping her coffee at the table overlooking the backyard, she watched a porcupine lumbering around. He had been chewing her trees for months now, and soon, she was told, the wood on her house would be next, and the tires on her car. She saw a chance to be the hunter. She bought a live trap.

She set it out in the backyard under the maple trees. She pulled fallen branches of green over the crate for camouflage. She tempted the animal by putting slices of apples, chunks of salt, and pieces of wood at the back of the trap, as she had researched on the Internet. She would not be the prey any longer. If she had to remain on this planet alone, it would not be in an all-consuming indignation, slowly pulling her body and mind into pieces. It was like porcupine quills were absorbing into her muscle tissue, causing endless agony. She fixed the spring on the top of the trapdoor and waited. She hoped for enough patience to get the job done quickly.

She looked out the window the next morning and saw the trapdoor had sprung shut. She saw the creature peering at her. She breathed deeply and approached the cage as the creature twisted and turned, trying to find a way out. It was heavy and awkward to carry to the car and lift inside. She drove in silence and refused to let any crippling thoughts enter her mind. After thirty miles, she turned onto a dirt road next to a sprawling coniferous forest. She parked and brought out the crate. She lugged the creature into the thick of the trees. The cage was tricky to unlatch. The creature was watching intently. There was no effort to hurt her now. She was the hunter. The door opened, and she stood back, watching as it waddled away without so much as a glance back, taking its spikes and heavy darkness farther and farther away, looking harmless and small. She trekked back to her vehicle, empty cage in hand. It was no effort to put it into the backseat now. She started the engine and sat, just sat. She wrapped her hands around the steering wheel and began driving toward home. For the first time, she turned on the radio and listened to a song without crying.

The trees on Primrose Street colour the sidewalks and gardens with painted leaves every autumn. Some residents rake and bag them into recyclable paper bags, leaving them on the curb for pick-up, while others leave them on their lawns for mulch during the winter months, and still others rake them into huge piles and children on the street make forts and tunnels. Some piles are so big that kids climb into the low maple branches and jump down into the leaf stacks. As the tree chuckles with delight at these goings-on, more leaves fall. This is a highlight of fall on Primrose Street, the piles of maple-leaf fun.

When winter comes and the trees shake themselves free of autumn, preparing themselves ready for the cold winds of a Canadian winter, their branches are slick and cold, making it difficult for children to climb. And then the sap begins to run, the tiny maple leaf buds begin to appear, and the birdsongs signal spring.

Mary keeps tending to her garden as the weather improves and often goes over to help Peter as he struggles to rebuild the garden in the front of his house. He initially just flattened everything out and put down fresh sod, but Mary has suggested some bushes. They go to a nursery together. Peter loves the butterfly bushes and the Rose of Sharon trees. He would like different shrubs and small trees, he tells Mary, no flowers. And so, they set out to create the garden for him, to welcome butterflies. They start with a few purple butterfly bushes. She is more than happy to help.

That spring, everyone on Primrose Street receives an invitation to Antonio and Phil's wedding. It comes in a cream-coloured envelope with a red-waxed seal on the back. The piece of paper inside is thick with importance. The writing on it is in a lovely cursive script, and the border is a collection of tiny trumpets. Ruth's hands shake when she sees the names and event on the invitation. She puts hers directly into the garbage and then takes it back out and puts a match to it in the sink along with Jessica's. She never tells Jessica.

Cheryl turns the envelope over and carefully slides a knife along the top edge, not wanting to break the gorgeous red wax seal. She slides the invitation out and just stands, the paper heavy in her hands, a tear smudging the handwritten message. She thinks of her Derek and how things could have been different. Her heart still aches to the point of collapse. So many moments missed. But there is so much hope and love in this tiny piece of elaborate paper. She doesn't waste a moment to get a pen, say yes, she'll be attending, slip it in the stamped envelope provided, and drop it in her purse, to be mailed the minute she can find her coat and shoes.

Phil and Antonio are getting married in Vancouver. Everyone on the street is invited. Cora looks at her invitation and remembers little Phil tucked up in the branches of the tree outside his house. She was never sure what he was doing up there, but she knew he was up there a lot. She tries not to think too much about things. The world is a rotating place, she tells herself, no point in trying to keep it still. She checks the blueberry pie she is baking and sits down at the table with the invitation. She looks at the two options on the card: attend, with or without a friend, not attending. She scribbles the pen on a scrap piece of paper beside her to make sure it was working and then, without hesitation, she checks the "attend with a friend" box. She'll just explain to Charlie on the way there.

Not everyone is so generous. Not everyone checks the "attend" box. Some don't even bother to return the invitation with an answer. Jessica does. Amiritha showed her the invitation. Her mother is aghast. She visibly pales when Jessica tells her.

"Mom, it's not their fault. It's not a choice they have."

"What are you saying? Of course, they have a choice."

"No, Mom, they don't."

"What about what he did to you, how can you ever forgive him for that?"

"Sometimes I'm still angry, sure. It broke me, almost killed me, and I almost killed others. But I don't want to live like that. I just don't."

"Some things are right, and some things are wrong, and that's that."

"Wasn't it wrong with Dad, Mom? Was your marriage perfect? No secrets?"

"That's different!"

"How, how is that different? At least Antonio and Phil aren't cruel and mean."

"Yes, they are, and they're liars."

"So was Dad. Why do you think John left? He literally ran away. Do you even know where he is? I mean Jesus, Mom, my own brother didn't even come to visit me in the hospital. Do you not know how fucked-up that is?"

"They are disgusting. What they do is disgusting."

"Did you hear what I just said? There's a lot of things that are disgusting, but that's not one of them."

"Oh my God, Jessica, what's wrong with you?"

"What's wrong with *you*, Mom? Open your eyes. When I was lying in that ICU, I had a lot of time to think. And yes, a lot of it was pretty gruesome thinking. But the therapist showed me other ways to think, and I realized it's all about moments. When we're inside one, it is virtually impossible to see beyond to another. Clinging too tightly may mean missing the next one. Or eliminating it completely. It's the ability to be surprised, to be available. No secrets."

"I can't believe you are actually going."

"Didn't you hear anything I just said?"

"This is all crazy."

"Maybe *you* should see that therapist, Mom."

"Don't you talk to me like that. I was the one that was here for you when everything fell apart."

"Yes, and thank you for that, but you weren't the only one, and I'm not in that place any more. Maybe you are."

"How dare you."

"You had no right to tear up my invitation, Mom."

"I was protecting you."

"I don't want that kind of protection. I want to be there for their moment. It's something I have to do."

"Well, I don't want to be there."

"Okay, fair enough."

"And I don't want to hear about it when you get back."

"If that's how you want to be, I can't stop you, clearly."

"Aren't you going to be late for work?"

"Yeah, I am." Jessica walks over and hugs her mom, who stands stiffly, pushing down her tears. Jessica turns, picks up her bag, and walks out the door, closing it softly behind her.

Justin and Amiritha say they will go with Jessica, along with Kevin. They all book their flight together.

Sam and Amanda know that their baby is coming soon, and she really shouldn't fly. But they feel one of them needs to be there. Sylvia says she isn't sure she wants to go without Sam.

"Is Dad going?" is the first thing she asks.

"Is Mom going?" asks Sam.

"I don't know, Sam. Frankly, I'm a little pissed at her too. Maybe it was easier for you, but it felt like everything I believed in was carried away in a rockslide. And I still struggle, I still struggle to know what everything means."

"I know, me too. You question what you believe in, and is it safe to believe in anything. I know Syl, I feel the same. Secrets are poison, but so are lies. I don't think Mom told us the whole story. I think it was her story. But I came back to live here. And really loving someone helps you to heal. And now we have a baby coming. It changes things."

"So, what of it."

"Well, I see Dad around, you know? I see how he has been treated. It's just all wrong. He has a story too. Mary seems to be the only one who listens. He's not a bad man, Syl."

"Have you talked to him?"

"No."

"There."

"But I'm thinking maybe we need to hear his side. I mean, look at Amanda, even she talked with her dad about Derek."

"Yeah, I heard how that turned out."

"What, through the gossip mill? I heard about it from Amanda. He listened, he recognized his part."

"Oh come on, Evan, he did not. He wouldn't change if he was hit by a Mack truck."

"Okay, maybe that's true. Cheryl basically kicked him out, but she was part of that too. I don't know, I just don't think it's all so neatly tied with a red ribbon. One size fits all, you know?"

"I guess."

"And dad wasn't a Robert, you know that. He was always there for us and for Mom too. How do we really know what happened between them, what went on behind closed doors, or didn't go on? How much did we really not know? Nobody really talked."

"People don't talk now."

"True, but Amanda and I talk. I learned how important it is. But for Dad, maybe it wasn't there. I don't know. But I sometimes wonder what happened that we didn't know about. Come on, Sylvia, he was at every one of your competitions, helped us with homework, took us on amazing trips every year."

"What are you doing, Sam? He fucking cheated on Mom, he cheated on all of us. And you still don't talk to him either. Fuck, don't lecture me."

"I will talk to him. Amanda and I have discussed this a lot. If people in her house had talked, Derek might still be here. I don't want things to end like this, like that. At the wedding, I'm going to talk to him. Try to start over. Hear him. I want to. I want him in my life. I miss him."

"I miss him too. I don't think Mom will come if he's there, but I do want to support Phil and Antonio. I mean, if Jessica is going, I really should go too. But Dad? I don't know, Sam."

"Okay, but don't wait too long. I'm just starting to open the door a crack, and that way I can see rather than trying to look through a solid object and see nothing."

"Fine, fine, I'll think about talking to him. And I'll come, just to shut you up. But I'm not promising anything. And don't get any ideas about us going up to him and having this great reunion. But I'll come. What about Amanda and the baby? Will you still come? I don't want to get out there and find out you changed your mind. I'll fucking kill you."

He laughs. "No, I'm going. Amanda can't fly when she's so close, but I don't think the baby will come until I'm back. She's not that far along. And if it does come sooner, I'll just fly back."

"What about Cheryl?"

"I think she feels she really needs to be there. I think it's a way of reconciling with Derek somehow. She's worried about leaving Amanda, but Sofia says she'll be there. She can't really afford to take her and Nicolas out west right now. She didn't really know Phil anyway. She's very sweet, so there will be someone here for Amanda."

"Okay, I'm glad. That's all good. Fine, I'll buy my ticket," says Sylvia. "I owe it to Jessica more than anything. I feel bad I've been so far away with everything that's happened to her."

"Awesome. I haven't seen you in a long time either. I'm glad you're coming."

"Okay, Evan, don't start getting all mushy on me."

"Send me a copy of your ticket."

"Hey!"

"Just kidding, sort of. Love you, sis."

"Love you too."

Charlie and Cora haven't been on a trip in years and have never been out west, so they have decided this will be a great opportunity, maybe their last big trip. They start researching hotels and day trips they can take part in. They want to make it a grand affair. Tabitha and her children all book their travel tickets together. Tabitha, who rarely talks to Maggie, calls her.

"So, what do you think about a gift?" she began.

"Yes, hello to you as well, Tab."

"Right, sorry. Hi. So, gift? I think we should all chip in and buy one thing. What do you think?"

"Before that, are Mom and Dad going?"

"Are you serious?"

"I guess that is a no. Didn't think Dad could get his head out of his ass long enough anyway."

"Jesus, Maggie."

"Oh, come on, Tab, you know how Dad feels about these things. Dad won't come because he's an asshole and Mom because she has no spine."

"That's a bit harsh."

"You know I'm right. Maybe someday we can have a real conversation. I don't know why you defend them. I really don't. Okay, so enough with the pleasantries, a gift. I just think it will be too hard to coordinate that with everyone. Do you want to do it?"

"Not really, thought you might."

"No thanks. If you aren't going to canvass the street, then let's just leave it and people will get their own gifts."

"Fine. Easier anyway. Okay, well we'll see you out there."

"Sure. Tab?"

"What."

"Want to get a coffee with me when we're out there? Hello? Tab, you still there?"

"Yeah, Mag, that would be good. Thanks."

"Okay. Bye."

"Bye." It is the first time in a long time that Tabitha doesn't feel alone. Maybe, just maybe, she will finally be able to tell someone her secret.

Susan and Joe decide not to attend. They will stay back with Ruth. And even as they settle into their decision, they feel a heaviness settle around them and are oblivious to the light spring breezes circling the maples.

BETWEEN HOUSES

She'd heard the stories. It was hard not to, living in Martineville. Everyone loved a juicy tale that could be twisted and corroded. That's what made it possible for others to stop thinking about their own calamities. Peter's story was chewed and launched onto the gossip freeway. Nothing seemed to surface that was interesting enough to replace it — yet. Of all the tales circulating, Mary wondered if any were even close to the truth. She sometimes wondered what really happened. No one ever seemed to care about that.

Peter could never run for office now. He'd accepted that. It was tough for him to get real estate listings these days. He thought about leaving town and starting somewhere else. The cement boots he seemed to be wearing made it hard to make any sudden moves or changes.

The announcement of Antonio and Phil's wedding was a bigger story than Peter's, juicier, something fresh to spin. Peter was finally free. Gossip has no reverse gear.

Mary was no stranger to debilitating thoughts or emotions. She was beginning to accept life without Graham. She had put some pieces of herself back together. She understood the journey of grief and could see how Peter struggled inside that dark hole. The town had isolated him, which was why she started helping him with the garden, in full daylight, for everyone to see. Something never felt right to her about the whole thing. The wasteland of a front yard that Rebecca left was an open wound for Peter. He didn't know where to start but wanted to replenish. He was so grateful for Mary's help and friendship.

He loved butterfly bushes. So they decided to plant three of them, all blooming in different colours. He didn't want any flowers or ornaments, just shrubs and bushes, he told her. So together they began researching different options: small flowering shrubs, small trees with multicoloured leaves like crotons, Brazilia Red Hots, Azalea Shiraz, Dracaena Colorama, maybe a Japanese maple. The search began. And they enjoyed the search. Peter would call Mary to say he'd found some plants at a nursery three hours away, and did she want to come. And off they would go. Mary would pack a snack for the drive. Choosing music for the car ride was fun because they both had a love of music. They began to listen more closely to the opposing music choices, enjoying the conversation sometimes more than the music. They'd eat at different restaurants, taste different wines, and laugh often. The nursery that weekend was large, and it was the Azalea Shiraz they were searching for.

"Mary, I think it's this one." Peter was crouched in front of a shining, colourful plant. Mary crouched down beside him. They both reached toward one of the extended leaves at the same time, their hands touching. The tingly shiver was unmistakable, but neither moved or showed the feeling. Their hands stayed in place while their tongues talked of how successful it would be in Peter's garden. They both stood in unison, their hands slipping to their respective sides. Mary put her hands into her jacket pockets, the blush on her cheeks camouflaged by the heat in the nursery.

They continued to visit nurseries, vineyards, and restaurants. Days and weeks passed and slipped into months. Mary continued to help Peter plant his new garden. The street watched, silently.

"Mary, I think I've found the Dracaena colorama. Care to join me this weekend?"

"That's exciting. Absolutely."

"It's a bit farther. I booked us two rooms at the hotel, because we'll probably have to stay overnight. I didn't think we needed to drive home tired."

"No right, good idea. I'll pay you for the room."

"Well, we can talk about that on the drive down. I'll pick you up at eleven tomorrow then? Oh, and bring a nice dress, they have some very fancy restaurants in this town you might like."

"Okay, see you tomorrow."

It was a long drive, and Mary was grateful to be staying overnight. Peter had booked a lovely hotel, and after finding the colorama, they went to the hotel to freshen up before dinner. Peter was waiting in the lobby when Mary came down.

"Happy birthday, Mary."

"How did you know, Peter?"

"I did my research." He handed her two tickets.

"Oh my god, these are tickets to *Tosca*. My favourite opera. How, how did you..." A tear slipped down her cheek.

Peter bent his arm and extended his elbow toward her. "Madam."

Mary smiled and took his arm. "Sir."

The opera was spectacular, as was the dinner. Peter had spared no expense. It was a perfect birthday, a perfect evening. As he held her hand, helping her into the car, she hesitated beside him. "Thank you," she said, and she leaned in to kiss his cheek before climbing into the car. For the first time, it was silent as they drove back to the hotel.

He kissed her, gently, in the elevator. His lips were soft and warm. She felt a heat rise inside her, and wanted to put her arms around him. The elevator doors opened, and they awkwardly adjusted clothing as other people entered the elevator while they exited. He put his arm around her waist, leading her through the door, and they embraced when the door closed behind them. He kissed her neck and she tipped her head to one side, inviting more caresses. They manoeuvred toward the bed slowly, as in a dance. He effortlessly pulled her dress over her head and pulled her close, unclipping her bra. She had a moment of NO; it was so new, it had been so long, Graham flashed through her mind, and yet she felt desire for Peter; she couldn't pretend otherwise.

They methodically undressed each other, pausing to appreciate each exposure, each moment of skin and touch and heat and longing. She had never experienced anything like Peter. He was incredibly tender and looked into her, found places that made her blush, touched her in ways she had never been touched except in her fantasies. And she became bold, wanting him like she had only imagined. He could be so raw and intense, so powerful, but in a way that brought her to him, made her crave him deeply. And he loved her hunger, the way she moved and wanted him. It was like being brought into the new world, stripped bare, exposed, the thrills racing through their bodies were dizzying. She clung to him. She wanted him over and over again. She felt like a teenager. She couldn't absorb him fast enough. He'd make her wait as he touched her imperceptibly, like dandelions in the wind, soft and ephemeral, and she'd cry out and push against his skin, feeling her breasts against him, and he'd move with her, around her, inside her. They were both lathered in each other's perspiration when they finally lay side by side, panting for breath. He rolled onto his side and kissed her neck, stroked her hair, and pulled her close to him. Tears soaked her pillow, silently spilling from the corners of her eyes, and she held him close, kissed his arms. They stayed like that as they slept. They rolled as one, never more than a breath from each other. Not a word needed to be spoken.

As the morning light seeped through the curtains, Peter held her close and whispered in her ear, "You are delicious." She smiled and pulled him closer, and they made love again. Finally, she lay on her back, arms behind her head, while he had his hand on her thigh, lying beside her.

"Peter."

"Yes."

"What really happened?" There was no movement. No breath. Just suspended moments as Peter considered.

"I was lonely, plain and simple."

"Was there a man involved, like the gossip tells?"

"Yes." He paused. "Okay. This is hard to explain."

"Try," she said.

"He was there. At work. I liked working with him. I wanted and needed physical attention. And someone I could trust, could talk to. And he was a good friend. We spent a lot of evenings working together before anything happened. I didn't seek it out, it just happened, and I didn't say no. One late work night over pizza and beer."

"Did you love Rebecca?"

"Yes."

"Do you still love her?"

"Maybe in some way, but she betrayed me. She abandoned me. She hurt me by never once hearing what I wanted to say. And before that by shutting me out. But I never felt for her what I feel for you. The way we make love never happened with her. Never. I never wanted her like you, and she never wanted me like you do. It's different. It's us."

"Do you still want a man now?"

"No. No, I don't. I never really wanted a man then. Not really. It was more the moment, the companionship. Have you never thought of being with a woman?" The question caught her off guard. Made her squirm a bit. He noticed. "And?"

"Yes. I guess so. Maggie and I have known each other a long time. We met at university. She is younger than me, but we always got along famously. It's why I came to Primrose Street in the first place. I can't say I never thought of lying with her naked. Seeing what her nipple would feel like in my mouth. Feels funny to say that out loud. But that's it, really. No more than that. I'm not turned on by a woman like I am a man, especially you. Your rawness mixed with tenderness is intoxicating." She paused. "I deeply loved Graham, you know that. He gave me back myself." Peter gently nodded. "He'll always have a piece of my heart. Always. Are you okay with that?"

"Yes, I'm okay with that. You two were wonderful together. I'm honoured that you want to be with me, Mary. I'm certainly not a Graham."

"No, you're you. And that's where we begin, with us."

"Yes, the beginning of us. I like that. Just to be clear, so you really get it, Terrell was just a really good friend with some benefits for those few times. That's it. That's all. " He paused, looking at her. "Thanks."

"For what?"

"For wanting to listen."

"How can it be any other way?"

"Well, it can. And I never want that again. Rebecca refused to hear, to understand, to talk."

"Is that why she left?"

"Yes, I guess so, I don't really know. She never listened, she never asked. She took her poisoned version, told that to the kids, and left. Everything we'd done together, everything we'd been together over the years seemed to amount to nothing all of a sudden. That is what I can't understand. What hurts the most. That none of that mattered. That there wasn't at least some kind of balance, an accounting. It all came down to just one moment. Not the millions of others."

Mary reached over and touched his face. He kissed her hand.

"I want to hear what you think, Peter. Know what you feel. And I want to say things deep inside me too."

"I want to hear." He leaned over and kissed her.

"What did this mean to you? Me, I mean." He rolled on his side and propped himself on his elbow, looking at her face.

"It means, you mean everything, Mary, everything and then some more." And he traced his finger along the side of her face.

"Peter."

"Yes."

"Do you know that I am falling in love with you?"

He lay back down on his pillow, looking at the ceiling.

"Do you know that it terrifies me to feel like this, because I don't know if I could lose you too," said Mary. "How do you feel?"

"Very close to you."

"You're scared of that word, love, aren't you?"

"Maybe. It just comes with baggage, I guess. And I don't want baggage between us. I want to start again. I will always have all my memories, I mean I was with Bec for twenty-five years, but I want this with you, Mary. I really do. I've always longed for what we have together."

"Me too."

"No secrets."

"No secrets."

Mary pulled him over to her and snuggled into his arm. They lay like that, just breathing and being together. It was more than enough.

When they returned to Primrose Street, there was a lightness about them, sunlight finding spaces between leaves to shine patterns. They spoke every day, in person, on the phone, by text. They began to talk of things outside Primrose Street, beyond their pain, into a world neither had thought was possible.

Antonio and Phil's wedding would only be a weekend, but Mary packed for a much longer trip, and so did Peter. When they boarded their flight to Vancouver, they had decided they would be continuing to Paris after the wedding. They each carried a one-way ticket to Europe, leaving the Monday after the wedding weekend. It was their adventure into the unknown, together.

Holding each other's hands and sitting in row six with a window seat on Flight 737 on route to Vancouver, their luggage tucked away beneath them, their small bags in the overhead bins, they smiled at each other. Peter leaned over and kissed Mary on the mouth, a kiss that lingered and lingered, and she sighed and stroked his face.

"Mary."

"Yes?"

"Before we go, there's something I need to tell you." He saw her face tighten. He moved closer to her so only she could hear his words.

"I love you."

The tall, mature maples have watched the residents of Primrose Street for almost a hundred years. They stand along the street, in front of homes, protecting backyards, some more gnarled than others. Their branches hang over lawns and shade driveways. They are climbing projects for children, homes for birds and squirrels. Some of their long limbs have been shamelessly amputated by hydro workers for electrical lines to run along the street unimpeded. A few of them have become hollowed by sadness and were taken down completely, unable to recover, their stumps used for planters and decorative art. They watch over the street, taking deep breaths as residents move through generations of families.

Amanda and Evan are beginning a new generation on Primrose Street. They have a baby boy. His name is Derek Peter. The piece of art that Kevin created is hanging on the wall over his crib. It's such a bright and happy piece. And they want their baby to know where his name came from. They never want Derek to be forgotten. Sometimes Cheryl takes it and puts it into her solarium. She is going to ask Jina to ask Kevin if he could paint them another one. Cheryl is collecting travel brochures. She's hoping for an adventure with her daughter.

Amanda and Evan had hoped that Charlie and Cora could do some babysitting, but Cora suffered a stroke when they returned from out west. Charlie was devastated. Everyone took turns taking him food because he didn't even know how to turn the stove on. He would just sit in Cora's chair, waiting for her to come home. And she did. Now she's teaching Charlie how to cook and look after their accounts, just in case.

Sofia and Nicolas practically moved in to help out when Cora was in the hospital. Nicolas and Charlie did a lot of colouring and got pretty good at Sorry and Jenga. Sofia found a full-time job at Graham's old bread shop and is training to be a baker. She never knew life could be so good.

And Daniel and Maggie are expecting next spring. They haven't told anyone just yet, except for Tabitha. It was her and Maggie's little secret together before they told the whole street. A secret for a secret, that's what they had said at their coffee out west. Maggie was looking forward to getting to know her nieces and nephew — and her sister.

Ronald Burke had taken his telescope to the top of one of the maple trees a number of years ago, hoping to see Santa. He is now an A student and wants to study astronomy at university. One of his teachers, Ms. Rothwell, couldn't be prouder. He still believes in Santa, and magic.

Jessica is teaching at the university now alongside Amiritha. She is finally working in her field. She underwent multiple surgeries, and now the burn marks are almost invisible along the side of her neck and face. She still misses Antonio, because for her it was never a lie when she fell in love. She would like to have someone special in her life, but her scars run deep. She rarely talks with her mother, who has taken a lot of the bird feeders down and doesn't like to miss Oprah.

Amiritha is now Mrs. Justin, that's what she likes to call herself. They sold the house next to the Burke's and bought a little house on the other side of town. They are planning their first trip to Pakistan, and Kevin couldn't be more excited.

Kevin does art with Jina quite often. It's now his full-time job. They have opened a gallery in town, that Kevin manages and curates, and he smiles a lot. Nicolas comes and helps out at the gallery. Kevin says he'll have a part-time job there pretty soon. He's becoming a pretty good artist himself. Jina keeps threatening to leave law for her art but just isn't quite ready. She also isn't quite ready to leave Primrose Street.

Mike finally left town, at Dayna's urging. No one knows where he went.

Antonio and Phil's wedding was beautiful, and everyone was proud to be a part of it. It was a small gathering of family and friends at a small venue near Stanley Park. The ocean sang at their backs. Antonio's mom and dad were there. They had found a way to come together and celebrate with their son. Phil's parents never really gave a good reason why they couldn't come, but Phil knew. He knew that place in his heart would always be bruised. But as he stood beside the love of his life, he thought about how far he'd come from sitting in the maple tree on Primrose Street. He had never even dared to dream the dream he was living.

Susan never forgave herself for not going, but she couldn't, she just couldn't. She had an inkling of Phil's ugly sexual preferences from an early age but didn't really want to know, had no idea what to do, so she just tried to keep washing it out of him. Her husband Joe just ignored the whole thing, like it never happened. If people mentioned it, he would change the subject. They were caught in the tangle of what is, what needs to be, and what could be possible; they were the knot in a fine necklace chain.

Joe and her never spoke of the wedding, and they rarely speak of Phil or to him.

Maggie got a postcard from every country Mary and Peter visited. They had decided to live on the island of Crete for a while. Peter just loved all the flowering bushes. Maggie and Mary would FaceTime each other often and follow each other on Facebook, and that's how Mary learned she was going to be a godmother soon. She told Maggie they had already bought their tickets for a visit home. Peter was speechless when he found out he had a grandson and that his second name was Peter. He broke down and wept. He was so glad to have his son back in his life. They talked often these days. And when he and Mary flew back to Primrose Street, Sylvia had agreed to a coffee.

The girls are planning their next luncheon. They will need a bigger table and many carafes.

The maple trees on Primrose Street lean and bend as the summer breezes waltz through their leaves; enchanting.

AUTHOR'S NOTE

I feel we have become very sanitized in our cultures today. We want things to be pretty and young and flawless. We give lip service to differences between us and struggles that exist in people's lives, but we prefer them to happen to everyone else. And so we really don't want to know, even it's right under our noses.

But this attitude, this approach, means that people keep secrets in order to fit in and exist with some element of contentment. But secrets are poison and they affect us all. I'm not a fan of mere lip service. I believe we have to really chew things in order to understand. Get the flavour, the experience. And as we are reluctant to do that, I wrote about it. Because to go forward, we need to step into each other's skin and find true empathy. I take people inside the ugly, the difficult, the pain, the humiliation ... and the joy. I expose the secrets. Show how they infect us all and then give some options. Options that can allow us all to live in our skin without secrets. To be free to be who we need to be.

Primrose Street is a microcosm of our society; anyone's street, or apartment complex, or condo tower, or community. It asks the reader to expand their perspective, reach out, be courageous, leave the sanitized, bleached comfort zone, and make our world a better place.

ABOUT MARINA L. REED

Marina grew up in rural Ontario. Her curiosity, passion, and desire to make a difference have taken her in many directions and to many parts of the globe. She holds a Hon.B.A., M.A., B.Ed. She has worked as a researcher and writer for CBC television programs, performed in theatre and film, has written in various print media, created online education programs, and taught liberal arts, visual art, and drama in public schools in rural and urban Ontario, Europe, and a developing country. Marina has been penning stories from a very young age and continues to document her journeys, observations, and experiences. Her hope is to stimulate thoughts, feelings, conversations and ideas in others and maybe facilitate positive change.

BOOK CLUB GUIDE

1. Sexuality is not a one-dimensional subject, and *Primrose Street* explores this concept. Have you ever had thoughts of being with someone of the same gender, and would you share those with your current spouse or partner? Why or why not?

2. Toxic masculinity is a recent phrase used to describe men who choose bravado and objectify women. What male characters would you say embody this description in *Primrose Street*, and why?

3. Do you hold a secret that could put you at risk? Who would you feel comfortable sharing it with?

4. Cora and Charlie have been together a long time. Name three things that you think are the reasons for the success in their relationship.

5. Rebecca had a very close relationship with a female friend. How did keeping that secret affect the way she handled Peter's affair? How could things have been different?

6. Why do you think Jessica walked into the fire? What does the fire symbolize?

7. Who are the men in the book that you would love to have a relationship with, and why? (This question is for the men and women in the room).

8. How did the story about Mary affect you in the way she dealt with the loss of Graham?

9. Many of our decisions about sexuality, partner choice, etc., are based on religious teachings. Religions that have killed millions in the name of God, debased women and taken away their rights, killed those who announce homosexuality and forced dysfunction in families to continue because of secrets kept. Do people like Derek and Phil not deserve to be authentic and exist freely? What are the unseen consequences of perpetuating a belief system that is flawed?

10. What was it that empowered Ronald to succeed in school? How can we give that to our own children?

11. Which woman do you identify with in *Primrose Street*, and why? (Again, men and women, what do you think?)

12. After reading *Primrose Street*, did you look at your neighbours differently? How would our communities change if everyone were to feel safe, respected, and honoured for who they really are and need to be?

WRITE FOR US

We love discovering new voices and welcome submissions. Please read the following carefully before preparing your work for submission to us. Our publishing house does accept unsolicited manuscripts but we want to receive a proposal first, and if interested we will solicit the manuscript.

We are looking for solid writing — present an idea with originality and we will be very interested in reading your work.

As you can appreciate, we give each proposal careful consideration so it can take up to six weeks for us to respond, depending on the amount of proposals we have received. If it takes longer to hear back, your proposal could still be under consideration and may simply have been given to a second editor for their opinion. We can't publish all books sent to us but each book is given consideration based on its individual merits along with a set of criteria we use when considering proposals for publication.

Thank you for reading *Primrose Street*

If you enjoyed *Primrose Street*, check out more
literary fiction from Blue Moon Publishers!

Beneath the Alders: The Innocent by Lynne Golding

To Love a Stranger by Kris Faatz